The Worst Lord in London

Scoundrels of Mayfair Book 1

ANNA CAMPBELL

Copyright © 2023 Anna Campbell

ISBN: 978-1-925980-26-4

All rights reserved. No part of this publication may be reproduced, distributed or transmitted in any form or by any means, without written prior permission.

Publisher's Note: This is a work of fiction. Names, characters, places, and incidents are a product of the author's imagination. Locales and public names are sometimes used for atmospheric purposes. Any resemblance to actual people, living or dead, or to businesses, companies, events, institutions, or locales is completely coincidental.

Cover Design: Hang Le

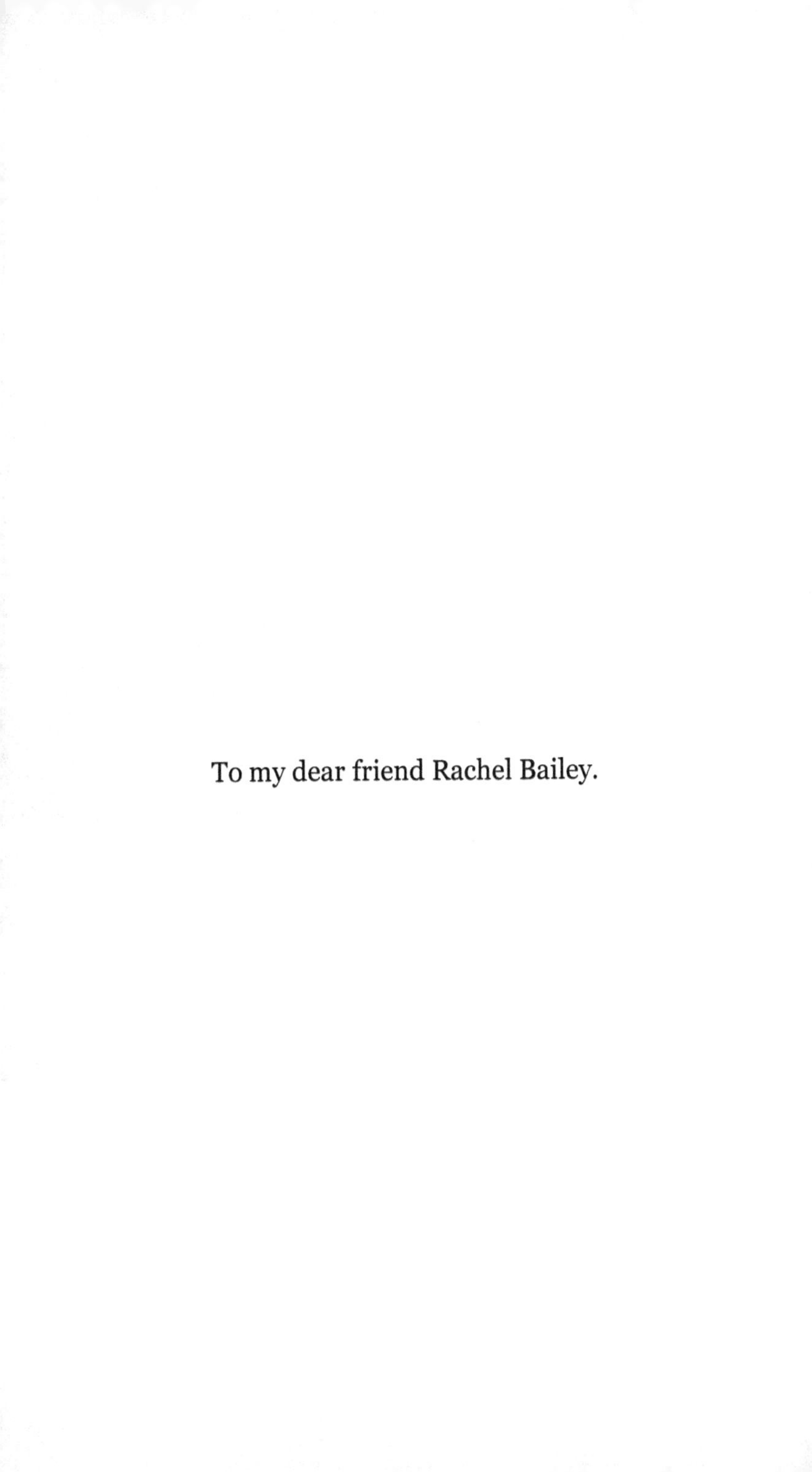

To my dear friend Rachel Bailey.

PROLOGUE

Rushby Hall, Lincolnshire, November 1802

When she was sixteen, Kate Starr fell in love. Forever.

Which was a surprise. In her family, she was considered hardheaded and practical. The type of girl who would never tumble willy-nilly into a hopeless infatuation.

But it turned out that she was that type of girl after all.

Of course, the object of her affections was handsome. Dazzlingly so. Like an archangel come down to earth. Lucifer before the Fall. Until now, her references had always tended toward much more earthbound beings. She wasn't at all imaginative or romantical.

Or she'd never before believed that she was.

She sat, to her relief ignored, on a spindly chair against the wall in Rushby Hall's gilded ballroom and watched the young man in question whirl her older sister around the floor in a waltz.

Hungrily she drank in the chiseled features and the shining black hair and the way his face lit up when he smiled at something Sylvie said. The flash of straight white teeth in that stark, medieval crusader's face made her untried heart clench in futile longing.

She'd never experienced a physical attraction before. Its power astonished her.

Kate wasn't alone in watching the dashing young nobleman and his ethereal partner. And to her regret, most of the attention wasn't kind.

"What on earth is Lemaire doing, dancing with that fright?" a cutting voice asked from several chairs along. Miss Phelps must know that Kate was within earshot, but she wouldn't give a fig for that.

In this aristocratic milieu, Sylvie and Kate were lowborn outsiders. From the moment that they joined the house party, they'd been made to feel their inferiority.

Sylvie was a school friend of Mary Rushby's. When Mary had invited Sylvie and Kate to visit the family estate for a ball to mark the start of foxhunting season, Kate's parents had been delighted to think that their daughters would have a taste of high society.

They'd have been less delighted to know that their daughters had been treated as pariahs from the first. A mill owner's children from Bradbourne in Derbyshire didn't belong among all these blue bloods.

"She's worth a fortune apparently," Miss Thwaites said in a bored tone.

"But Lemaire doesn't need to marry for money. When he inherits the Shelburn earldom, he'll be one of the richest men in England."

Praise for The Worst Lord in London:

"I loved this. I was so glad that we got to properly meet Kate Starr whom we caught only a glimpse of in previous release, *Two Secret Sins*. She was intriguing then and proves to be even more so now. *The Worst Lord in London* has all the Campbell hallmarks – it's sexy, our rake hero is utterly gorgeous, and the heroine is clever, courageous and more than a match for him. Fabulous." ***Cathryn Hein, bestselling author of* The Country Girl**

"This was a well-written, nicely paced story with wonderful characters and more emotion than I was expecting! The book is steamy and satisfying, with great secondary characters, a sinister plot twist, a hero who claims he is not a knight in shining armor (but who really is), and finally a very sweet HEA." ***Flippin' Pages Book Reviews***

"I liked both of them and loved how their relationship unfolded. It was a surprise to both of them and felt fresh and highly romantic. I really enjoyed their story and this new series is off to a great start." ***Blue Mood Café***

"Another fabulous story from one of my favourite authors, Anna Campbell, she has a beautiful way of telling a story and this one is sensual and sizzling as we see the worst lord in London lose his heart to the most beautiful of innocents." **5 stars. *Romance Book Haven***

"Once again Ms. Campbell brings her lovely, deeply developed characters to us. Seeing each of them as they think through their reaction to the instant attraction and deep connection they feel was wonderful. The humor and fun banter makes this a page turner. Thank you for a splendid read, Ms. Campbell." ***Buried Under Romance***

"I utterly loved this book. Anna knows how to write characters you adore and stories that pull you in!" **5 stars. *Amazon Reviewer***

"I loved, loved their story. It was filled with heat but plenty of sweetness. And their epilogue is the cherry on top of the sundae. Just a perfect read that left a smile on my face." **5 stars. *GoodReads Reviewer***

"The reader will be captivated by the story about a successful woman in a world ruled by men, and of a man whose life has nothing more to offer apart reckless behavior and mindless dalliances. Nobody knows how to write about seduction and lovemaking like Anna Campbell." **5 stars. *GoodReads Reviewer***

"Smart, sexy romance. Anna Campbell is at her best when writing about dissolute rakes and resourceful women. Kate and Leighton's story will make you laugh, seethe with outrage and ultimately, sigh with satisfaction." **5 stars. *GoodReads Reviewer***

ALSO BY ANNA CAMPBELL

Claiming the Courtesan

Untouched

Tempt the Devil

Captive of Sin

My Reckless Surrender

Midnight's Wild Passion

The Sons of Sin Series:

Seven Nights in a Rogue's Bed

Days of Rakes and Roses

A Rake's Midnight Kiss

What a Duke Dares

A Scoundrel by Moonlight

Three Proposals and a Scandal

The Dashing Widows Series:

The Seduction of Lord Stone

Tempting Mr. Townsend

Winning Lord West

Pursuing Lord Pascal

Charming Sir Charles

Catching Captain Nash

Lord Garson's Bride

The Lairds Most Likely Series:

The Laird's Willful Lass

The Laird's Christmas Kiss

The Highlander's Lost Lady

The Highlander's Defiant Captive

The Highlander's Christmas Quest

The Highlander's English Bride

The Highlander's Forbidden Mistress

The Highlander's Christmas Countess

The Highlander's Rescued Maiden

The Highlander's Christmas Lassie

A Scandal in Mayfair Series:

One Wicked Wish

Two Secret Sins

Three Times Tempted

Four Christmas Kisses

Scoundrels of Mayfair Series:

The Worst Lord in London

The Trouble with Earls

The Last Duke She'd Marry (2023)

The Duke Says I Do (2024)

Christmas Stories:

The Winter Wife

Her Christmas Earl

A Pirate for Christmas

Mistletoe and the Major

A Match Made in Mistletoe

The Christmas Stranger

His Christmas Cinderella (in the anthology A
Grosvenor Square Christmas)

Other Books:

These Haunted Hearts

Stranded with the Scottish Earl

"Perhaps he's decided one can never have enough money. Although I'm sure he won't tarnish the family escutcheon by marrying into trade."

"Well, why else would he waste time with that frump?"

Kate bit her lip and battled the urge to tell the two hoity-toity harpies to shut their spiteful traps. She wanted to tell them that her sister was lovely. Sweet and funny and clever. And she'd been so looking forward to this party. Kate didn't much care that most of the guests despised her, but she cared that they were mean to Sylvie.

Sylvie, who had been well enough to attend this gathering, in a way that she hadn't been well for the last two years. Sylvie, who did care that the other girls shunned her and the gentlemen snickered about her unfashionable appearance and provincial manners.

Sylvie, who had imagined that this ball would be glamorous and exciting and fun. Yet who had sat wilting with disappointment, as dance after dance went by with no young man offering to partner her.

Until Viscount Lemaire had crossed the room and asked her for the first waltz. Kate had heard enough gossip over the course of the visit to know that the young viscount was considered a catch and an arbiter of taste. His approval meant a great deal in this elevated society.

Now, thanks to his kindness, Sylvie was dancing with one of the most admired young men in England. Her thin face was alight with happiness.

Yes, Lord Lemaire was handsome enough to make a girl's heart beat faster. But Kate was too sensible to fall in love with mere good looks.

What stole Kate's heart away between one breath and the next was that Lord Lemaire had looked across at Sylvie sitting alone and ignored, and he'd taken the trouble to do something about that.

Kate could resist masculine appeal. But the man who made her sister smile, who was kind enough to take pity on Sylvie's plight, that was a man worth loving.

CHAPTER ONE

The Angel, Islington, London, May 1816

"My goodness me, what a to-do," Cousin Hazel twittered, all aflutter as she minced out of the inn where they'd stayed last night before completing the final leg of their journey this morning. Around them, the yard was crammed with a heaving, vociferous crowd and a battalion of expensive carriages.

"It was busy last night," Kate said, stepping sharply out of the way as a pair of urchins darted past, shrieking with excitement. She tightened her hold on her reticule. She'd been to London before, and she didn't intend to lose another purse to pickpockets.

"Not like this." Hazel flapped her hand in front of her face, as if to save herself from swooning. Kate ignored the movement. Hazel often acted as if she might faint. She never did.

"Where the devil is our coachman?" Alfred Mercer, Hazel's husband, said in his grumpy fashion as he came up behind them. "I'd imagined a Sunday morning might be a little quieter. Especially at this hour. It's not even eight. All these people should be in church."

"Why?" Kate cast Alfred a disdainful glance. He wasn't her favorite person in the world. "We're not."

As usual, Alfred ignored her. She wasn't his favorite person either. He snatched the arm of a passing tradesman. "My good sir, what's going on here?"

The noise around them was cacophonous, and Kate saw the man take a moment to translate Alfred's flat northern vowels into something that he could understand. "It's a race. From here to Hatfield. To win the favors of Lady Verena Gerard."

"What an appalling example to set for the lower orders."

It was clear that the man wanted to get back into the thick of things, instead of dallying here with three provincial nobodies. "Just a bit of fun, guvnor."

Alfred sniffed in disapproval. "Who is racing?"

But Kate's sharp eyes had already worked out the astonishing answer to that question. The yard's din receded, drowned under the blood pounding in her ears.

She found herself staring at a flashy red and black high-perch phaeton that contained someone who she hadn't seen in fourteen years. Someone who, unlike that dour bore Alfred, topped her list of favorite people.

Shelburn...

She straightened, afraid that she might have spoken the word aloud.

Reminding herself that she was in public, she dragged herself back to the present. But to her relief, nobody paid her any attention at all.

So Kate took advantage of the moment to eat up the sight of Leighton Anstey, Earl of Shelburn. Stupid, stupid to be giddy with happiness. It was no more than an extraordinary coincidence that their paths crossed today of all days.

He was as handsome as ever, if no longer the angel-faced boy she remembered. How could he be? Fourteen years meant that he was now a man of thirty-two. Kate had changed over that time, too, thank heaven. At the very least, she was no longer plump and spotty and awkward.

Shelburn hadn't devoted the years to rescuing damsels in distress either, she knew, although plenty of damsels had featured in his life. She subscribed to most of the gossipy London papers, so she'd followed his profligate career after he'd inherited his father's title at twenty-four. He'd cut a wide swath through the ladies of the ton, not to mention a bevy of less respectable females from the demimonde.

Thanks to those newspapers, she knew exactly who Verena Gerard was as well. London's wildest lady – or at least the wildest one who remained acceptable to society.

When a woman bowled in, driving a cabriolet, Kate had no trouble recognizing Lady Verena from illustrations in the papers. Recent press indicated that Lady Verena was more than just a wild lady. She was also the woman who had captivated Shelburn's wandering attentions. At least for the moment.

The agonizing surge of jealousy was the strongest emotion that Kate could remember feeling in years. Childish and useless as it was. This glimpse of the man whose memory she'd cherished was nothing but a cruel reminder of impossible dreams from the past and the unappealing choices available to her in the present.

Sensible choices. Safe choices. And not one spark of joy in any of them. Plague take it.

Because while she stood here about to step into the next phase of her life, Lord Shelburn would dash out of her world forever in pursuit of another lady. A lady who was glamorous and highborn and exciting in a way Kate could never be.

It was enough to make her want to kick something. But calm, prudent, clever Kate Starr would never make a public scene. For heaven's sake, this distress was inefficient, and inefficiency was anathema to a canny mill owner from the rough north.

So instead of expressing her violent emotions, she stood hiding chagrin and regret, while Alfred and Hazel talked around her but not to her.

Kate watched Lady Verena consign the cabriolet to her groom and join an elegant, yellow-haired man in a sporting curricle. Lady Verena bristled with visible fury. Even through Kate's fug of shock and envy, she could understand that no lady wanted to have her name bandied around a common innyard.

"We're going to be so very, very late," Hazel fussed from beside her. "I can't imagine what Mr. Williams will think."

"He'll think that we were held up through no fault of our own." Kate's tone was repressive, as every absurd hope that she'd ever harbored in her secret heart shriveled and died.

Because after all these years, she was within reach of the man whose memory had haunted her. Yet he still might as well be a million miles away.

He'd go on from here to seduce Verena Gerard and probably a hundred other pretty ladies, while Kate accepted the uninspiring future that she'd fought against for so long.

That reality was more painful, now that she'd snatched this brief glimpse of Shelburn. It was as though Fate snickered at her powerlessness, much like those nasty cats had laughed at her so long ago at Rushby Hall.

"Come inside until the crowds have dispersed." Hazel placed her lavender-gloved hand on Kate's arm. "I can't think it's respectable for us to stand out here in public, gawking at such disreputable goings-on."

"You're right, my dear," Alfred said. "If we give these drunken louts the benefit of our attention, it only encourages their depravity."

Kate bit back a retort that no person here gave a snap for what three nobodies thought of the aristocracy's antics. Even if she and her companions stood on their heads and sang "Rule, Britannia!" backward, not one soul would spare them a glance. All eyes were on the race's participants. By now, the two carriages were lined up together, ready to set off.

But as she turned to go back into the inn, something made her pause to glance at Shelburn. One last look at what had always been an unattainable fantasy, even if it almost hurt more to see him than not. She felt old and despondent, as she relinquished the last vestiges of her foolish penchant. Because even futile dreams added a spark to life.

Now she had no dreams left at all.

Shocked into immobility, she realized that not every scrap of attention was fixed on the two carriages about to head for Hatfield. Instead, Lord Shelburn's unreadable dark stare leveled on her.

All of a sudden, the heart that had felt as heavy as lead revived to frantic life and crashed into her ribs, stealing her breath.

"Kate?" Hazel asked from the doorway, as she realized that her cousin lagged behind.

Kate's eyes met Shelburn's. Even across the distance, she felt the force of that sharp gaze. The breath jammed in her throat as something inside her insisted that this very second, her life was about to change forever.

If she was brave enough to step up to the challenge.

"You." Shelburn pointed the handle of his whip straight at Kate. "The pretty miss in the blue dress over there."

Kate released her pent-up breath in a gasp. Something daft and female inside her blossomed to hear him say that she was pretty. The chaotic activity around her faded to nothing. All she knew was that the man she'd cherished in secret had noticed her at last.

An expectant silence fell over the crowd. Now everyone was looking at her, with no singing or acrobatics required.

Shelburn went on without waiting for a response. Which was fortunate, because the capacity for speech had abandoned her. "Do you fancy a bit of excitement this morning? You look about Verena's size. What about a trip to Hatfield? I'll see you're escorted right and proper wherever you want to go afterward, and throw a gold necklace into the mix to make it worth your while."

He must be trying to even up the weights of the two vehicles, now that Lady Verena rode with his opponent. Kate shouldn't even consider saying yes. There was her reputation to consider. If she set off alone with such a notorious seducer, it would be in ruins.

"What do you say?" As if he sought a better view of her, he tipped back the brim of his hat with the whip handle. "It will be a story you can tell the grandchildren over the fireside, when you're old and gray. About the day you helped a rake to win a race for another lady's heart."

What on earth was wrong with her? She'd made plans for the rest of her life. If she did this mad thing, they'd collapse in a heap around her feet. Even more discouraging, Shelburn had just confirmed that his interest lay with Lady Verena.

"I'll come with you, Shelburn," a stout, middle-aged lady called out from the crowd.

Kate cast her a quick glance. Was she wearing a ball gown? This day became stranger by the minute.

The man next to her, also in evening dress, gave a jeering laugh. Kate assumed that he was the lady's husband. "Emily, you're twice Verena's size. Don't be a goose."

The nasty note in the general laughter that greeted this ungallant remark again reminded Kate of that horrid house party at Rushby Hall. At sixteen, she'd been too cowed to speak to the man who caught her eye. Now she had a second chance to make her mark with the louche Earl of Shelburn.

It was time for daring, not propriety. That thought banished the last of her indecisiveness.

She stepped forward and when she spoke, her voice was calm and carrying. "I'd be delighted to come, my lord."

He didn't look surprised. The earl must be used to women doing what he wanted.

"Kate, don't you dare!" Hazel bleated behind her. Perhaps this time, she might faint.

Kate didn't even look back, as she marched up to Shelburn's carriage and held out a hand for him to help her into the seat.

"Good for you, miss." The smile that curled that expressive mouth was everything wicked and forbidden. A reminder that this was no longer the picturesque youth who had danced with Sylvie. This man's name was a byword for everything that people warned innocent girls to avoid.

The smile was irresistible. *He* was irresistible.

His hand closed around hers. He'd never touched her before. Given that they both wore gloves, he wasn't really touching her now. But at the contact, a surge of heat unlike anything in her experience blasted Kate.

As a woman in a man's world, she'd become used to hiding her emotions. Through habit, she concealed the turbulent storm of excitement and doubt raging inside her. With ease, she climbed up to sit beside Shelburn. She was an active, agile woman, used to long walks over the moors near her home.

The seat was narrow, and her hip pressed against his in a way that set her asinine heart skipping. Her gaze skimmed the crowd. Alfred looked ready to explode. Hazel was pale with shock. Kate caught surprise and curiosity and even admiration on the other faces.

Apart from her cousins, nobody here knew her. But the spectacle of a respectable female placing herself in a rake's power was enough to set tongues wagging.

"Call off the race, Eliot," Lady Verena said to the man sitting beside her in the curricle.

Lord Colville smiled at his passenger as if she'd hung the stars in the sky. He was as golden as Apollo, such a contrast to dark and sardonic Shelburn. "It's too late."

"Are you ready now, my lords?" the landlord asked from the box that he stood on to be visible above the throng.

"I am," Shelburn said, as calmly as if he set off on a stroll in Hyde Park.

The innkeeper turned to the other carriage. "Lord Colville?"

"Eager to go, landlord," the blond man said with matching sangfroid.

Once again Shelburn touched the brim of his stylish high-crowned hat, this time in a salute to his rival. "Good luck, Colville. May the best man win."

"Make way. Make way." The landlord raised a large white handkerchief. "Good luck, my lords. Ready. Set. Go! And God save the King!"

The handkerchief fluttered to the ground. A mighty cheer rose from the onlookers. Shelburn's carriage lurched into motion a fraction ahead of the curricle.

Her pulses pounding with an anticipation that had very little to do with the race, Kate clenched one hand over the metal railing on the side of the carriage. She placed her other hand on her bonnet to keep it in place as the pace picked up. With dizzying speed, Lord Shelburn's carriage rattled away from the Angel and onto the busy streets.

CHAPTER TWO

o Shelburn's relief, the handsome woman at his side remained silent as he wove his way through the traffic outside the Angel. Even on a Sunday morning, the streets were packed and chaotic.

They'd made a better start than Colville, whose high-strung grays had taken longer to settle than the chestnuts. Shelburn had no doubt, though, that once they hit the open road, Colville's team would give him some real competition.

It turned out that his companion was a wise choice. The woman didn't shriek or giggle or squirm in her seat. In fact, her self-possession struck him as damn near inhuman. He could be sitting beside a pretty porcelain doll.

Except even through concentrating on his driving, his masculine instincts continued to operate. He was infernally aware of the soft friction of her hip against his and her skin's subtle floral perfume. His companion might be quiet, but she was all woman.

Only after he'd paid the toll at Highgate did he at last have a chance to satisfy his rising curiosity about the lady who had accepted his outrageous invitation. She was without doubt a lady. Her manners were excellent. Her accent was educated. Her clothing was in the first stare.

Which deepened the mystery.

Females of such obvious quality didn't in general flit off alone in a noted rake's company. Not unless they were prepared to sacrifice their good name.

When he'd singled her out in the crowd at the innyard, he'd been giving his audience something to talk about and living up to his reputation as a shocking fellow. You could have knocked him down with a feather when she'd straightaway taken him up on his improper challenge.

He checked behind him, but there was no sign of Colville and Verena. The viscount must still be snarled up in the traffic. Shelburn eased back on the reins and let the chestnuts settle into a steady run that would cover the twenty miles to Hatfield in good form. The road ahead was clear, so he could see no impediments to making excellent progress.

With more purpose, he turned to regard the woman beside him. This time, he had the luxury of taking in the details of her appearance. She was lovely – he'd noticed that already. In an understated manner that appealed to a man jaded with flashier attractions. That blue ensemble clung to her elegant curves. The body under that modish pelisse promised to be spectacular.

She was tall, too. In the innyard, she'd towered over her two companions.

He checked the road ahead – no traffic in sight. The next time he glanced at his passenger, she was staring out at the fields alongside them with a calm attention that he began to find a little annoying. Here she was at the mercy of a man with a devilish reputation, and she was as serene as a girl taking tea with a maiden aunt.

By God, he was nobody's maiden bloody aunt.

For a long moment, he studied that perfect profile. A marked dark brown brow. A straight, rather determined nose. An equally determined chin. Two pink lips hinting that all the determination might float on top of a hidden sea of warmth.

The corners of those beguiling lips tightened, and a tinge of color brightened her creamy complexion. "You're staring, my lord," she said, her voice deep for a woman's.

He should apologize. He didn't. "I am."

When she faced him, he found himself staring into beautiful hazel eyes, framed by thick dark lashes. Two wings of sable hair parted over her forehead before they disappeared under her concealing bonnet.

This was no ingenue. She might even be close to his own thirty-two. But by heaven, she was a peach. While she was a change from his usual fare of flighty widows and temperamental actresses, she was delicious all the same.

"I should introduce myself," she said with more of the self-possession that both intrigued and piqued him. He was an infamous libertine who made debutantes swoon away with terror – or excitement. Why in Hades was his enticing passenger so calm?

"At the very least."

She ignored his jibe. "My name is Kate Starr."

Kate Starr? It was a plain name – if one didn't start thinking of the heavens. It suited her.

He frowned. "I don't know any family by that name."

The smile that lengthened her lips held a hint of cynicism. No, this was no foolish innocent. Her features expressed intelligence and an ease with herself that he found disconcerting. The only other woman he could think of who seemed as comfortable in her own skin as this one was Verena. But Verena's turbulent spirit seemed alien to this poised creature.

"The Starrs are well beneath a nobleman's notice, my lord."

He responded in a manner that was just as dry. "I doubt you were brought up in a hovel. That dress cost a pretty penny."

"We're mill owners from the north. Rich but not refined."

"Solid, hardworking folk."

"Yes. Not at all the sort of people to make a spectacle of ourselves with a public race."

"Yet here you are."

"Here I am."

He waited for her to explain her presence, but her eyes sharpened on him. "Are you sure this is the best way to win the lady's heart? When we left London, Lady Verena seemed furious with you. After this, I can't imagine she'll look on your suit with favor."

He shrugged with a carelessness that he didn't have to pretend. "She'll forgive me. We've been friends since we were children."

"So if you win, she agrees to marry you?"

With a half-horrified laugh, he adjusted his hold on the reins. "Good Lord, Miss Starr, I hope not. I'm in no hurry to fall into the parson's mousetrap. Colville has put those spectacular grays of his on the line. If I win, they're mine. If he wins, I've promised to stay away from Verena."

A frown drew Miss Starr's brows together. "And Lady Verena has no say in the outcome?"

"I suspect she has a great deal to say, but luckily right now, she's saying it to Colville." Something prickled at his awareness. "Is it *Miss* Starr?"

"Yes."

"That's good." Shelburn smiled, as he urged the horses on past a lumbering wagon piled high with hay. "I wouldn't like to think there was a Mr. Starr."

He waited for her to question his statement, but she just responded with more of that blasted serenity. "I owe nobody my obedience, my lord."

She was a strange female, independent and plainspoken and confident. And unlike most of the women of his acquaintance, she wasn't fluttering around trying to attract his notice.

Shelburn wasn't sure how he felt about that. Most of the time, he found tinkling laughter and blushes and eyelash batting a deuced nuisance.

He'd be the first to admit that his success with the fairer sex had left him spoiled. But something about Miss Starr's unshakable coolness irked him. However contrary the wish, he'd dearly love to see her a little flustered in his presence. At the very least, it would indicate that he didn't suffer this powerful attraction alone.

Because he was attracted. More than he could remember feeling in years.

"Why did you accept my invitation?" he asked, once the road ahead was clear and he could devote his attention to her.

"There's not a lot of adventure in Bradbourne," she said, maintaining that dry note. "As you said, it's a story I can tell my grandchildren."

"Bradbourne? Is that where you're from?"

"Yes, it's in Derbyshire."

"And your family owns a cotton mill?"

"To be more accurate, *I* own several cotton mills. I inherited the business when my father passed away."

At least some of her self-assurance came from wealth, he realized. "So you're *very* rich."

"But still not refined."

He gave a theatrical sigh. "And I see in no humor to flirt with an unregenerate cad. When I saw you across that innyard, I had hopes of luring you into a tryst."

To his surprise, his mention of dalliance ruffled her and at last he got his wish. She blushed as red as a tomato, and her gaze flickered away from his. "For shame, my lord. You shouldn't say that when you're devoting your Sunday morning to a mad dash to win Lady Verena Gerard's favors."

"I'm in pursuit of a new pair to pull my carriage, rather." Shelburn took pity on her and allowed her to gather her composure. Flicking the reins, he stared over the backs of his galloping horses for a few seconds. "If you feel the need to flirt, you're not stepping on anyone's toes. Verena has no prior claim."

"Oh."

Interesting that Miss Starr didn't deny that she hankered after a flirtation. He'd just given her the ideal opportunity to tell him to get back into his box.

His busy mind turned over this odd conversation. He remained puzzled about what had brought her here, but he developed a suspicion that she harbored improper intentions toward him.

How very satisfactory.

A vehicle rattled up behind him at a cracking speed. "Hold on. I think the competition is about to heat up."

Shelburn had been right about those grays putting on a kick, once they got out of London. Just now, his unsuitable surmises about his companion had to take second place to steering his rig. It would be a blasted shame if Miss Starr didn't survive the trip to Hatfield. He wanted to follow up on that intriguing hint of willingness.

She hooked one hand over the edge of the carriage as it bounced along the road. Shelburn urged his chestnuts on, but despite his best efforts, the curricle soon drew level with his phaeton.

Because he was thoroughly enjoying himself, he even found it in him to smile at a man who had never been a friend. "I see you've woken up, Colville. About time."

"Just lulling you into a false sense of security, old man," Colville replied, his grays laboring all out to pass Shelburn. For a chap with such a staid reputation, Eliot Ridley was proving quite the whip.

For a few breathless moments, the carriages raced together. Then second by second, Colville drew ahead until he was in the lead and driving well in front.

"That was a pretty piece of driving." Excitement vibrated in Miss Starr's voice.

"Thank you."

"No, I meant Lord Colville."

Shelburn burst into laughter. "Don't spare my feelings."

"I won't," she said, calm as ever, while Colville's carriage took the hill ahead at an impressive clip. The distance between the two vehicles widened by the second. "Aren't you going to try and catch up?"

Shelburn's hands remained loose on the reins. "I don't think so."

She frowned. "I don't understand."

Trying not to smile, he glanced at her. "You will in time, I suspect, if those two stubborn idiots ahead can come to some agreement." He paused. "And I say that with the greatest respect."

He watched realization seep into Miss Starr's fine hazel eyes. "You don't want to win the race?"

"I don't."

"So you're not pursuing Lady Verena?"

"I told you I wasn't."

Humor lit her expression, and she gave him the same response that he'd given her when she told him she had no husband. "That's good."

Pleased surprise jolted him. He drew the horses back to a walk and shifted on the seat so that he could meet her gaze. "Miss Starr—"

She put her hand up. "Can we...can we wait until we get to Hatfield before I tell you why I'm here?"

For a long interval, he surveyed her. From the first, her actions had puzzled him, although he knew now that she was drawn to him, too. She didn't carry on like a giddy girl, but he read an interest to match his own in those lovely eyes.

"Given we're only half an hour away from the end of the race, I'm prepared to wait." He paused. "Although now I'm cursing the fact that I have to let that self-righteous prig Colville win. My incentive for a speedy trip has just increased to infinity."

Miss Starr's laugh was an appealing sound. "The viscount doesn't strike me as a self-righteous prig. He seems a rather dashing fellow, and he handles the ribbons like a master. In fact, I doubt if a self-righteous prig would enter such a race in the first place."

Shelburn smiled, accepting that if they were to have the conversation that awaited – and act upon it, he very much hoped – he needed to be patient.

His deepest instincts assured him that the wait would be worth it.

"You know, I'm probably not being fair to Colville. Over recent weeks, he's proven himself far from a bore. I'm sure he remains too holy to associate with my sinful self, but as he's about to marry my best friend, we'll both have to declare a truce."

Shelburn watched Colville crest the next hill at a furious pace. At this rate, he wouldn't have to try too hard to lose, although he suffered a brief, unworthy pang when he acknowledged that those magnificent thoroughbreds would never find a place in his stables.

He just hoped to hell that Verena and her unlikely suitor made good use of their time together and found some common ground. He'd hated seeing her so unhappy this season.

"You're a good man," Miss Starr said in a low voice.

"No, I'm not." Something in her tone grated. Shelburn shifted on the seat and urged the chestnuts to a gentle canter that offered no hope of overtaking Colville and Verena.

"I know what I see."

His response emerged with a sharpness that worked against his seductive intentions. "Don't start looking for qualities that aren't there, or you're asking for trouble."

Her gaze remained steady. "I'm asking for trouble anyway."

Yes, she was. And he was the last man to try and talk her out of it. With every minute in her company, his desire grew more unruly.

Did she see that he was in a fever to have her? What else did she see?

Those eyes were so clear and perceptive. Most of the time, his conquests didn't look beyond the surface. He couldn't help feeling that Miss Starr saw past his famous social polish to the yawning emptiness within. Perhaps he was asking for trouble, too.

CHAPTER THREE

It was mortifying quite how glad Kate felt to hear that Lord Shelburn wasn't pursuing Lady Verena Gerard.

But that knowledge made her more aware than ever that this mad, scandalous adventure promised to lure her into very deep water indeed. An impulse too urgent to ignore had made her accept Shelburn's invitation. But as the carriage rattled across the miles toward her encounter with destiny, she had time – too much time – to wonder how all of this might play out.

As Shelburn kept up a steady pace along the road, Kate's sensible side nagged at her to take him at his word and leave him once they reached Hatfield. He'd offered her transport to anywhere she wanted after the race. She could go back to Hazel and Alfred.

On her return to London, a scolding awaited, but she'd survived those before. She'd survive this one. After all, her cousins relied on her for the roof over their heads, which gave her the final say in what she did. They might disapprove of her actions, but in the end, Kate was a free agent.

Nor did Kate's uncharacteristic behavior need to alter her immediate plans. However imprudent this carriage ride with Shelburn might be, she was sure that she could talk her way back into Mr. Williams's good books. After all, while Kate might have a pristine reputation, at least to date, that wasn't the principal reason for her suitor's interest.

Even if Shelburn cut up rough about letting her go, once they arrived at the Greyhound, she had plenty of money in her reticule. She could hire a carriage on her own behalf. A woman of means needn't be at anyone's mercy, unless she wanted to be.

Unless she wanted to be...

That was the crux of the issue, wasn't it? For most of her life, her sensible side had held sway. The one romantical thing that she'd ever done was fall in love with an aristocratic stranger.

Until today, when she'd accepted an invitation that wasn't at all the usual thing in her busy, purposeful, practical life.

Kate was no ninnyhammer. Despite all her girlish fantasies, she was well aware that she didn't know Lord Shelburn. He might have once done a kind thing. That didn't mean he was a kind man.

Except that it was clear he was doing something kind for Lady Verena and Lord Colville. Despite not particularly liking Colville. Was it possible that her sixteen-year-old self hadn't been so far off the mark with her starry-eyed assessment?

Only a woman of uncommon bravery – or recklessness – would risk safety and reputation on such frail evidence. Far safer to scuttle back to London and follow through on her plans, no matter how little personal fulfillment they promised. Safety had always been her guide, and she'd prospered as a result.

"I can almost hear your mind whirring," Shelburn said dryly from beside her. That lazy drawl was new since they'd last met. She had to keep remembering that in the time between, this man had lived a life she could hardly imagine.

While prudence had ruled Kate's every action, he'd indulged in debaucheries beyond her comprehension. No attractive woman was safe from him, if she was to believe the stories. And after more than an hour in his company, she did believe them.

Goodness, even his voice dripped with seduction. That deep, sardonic baritone seeped into her very bones. No wonder all those ladies had succumbed. Everything about him promised to deliver pleasure.

Kate had never known pleasure. Not the sensual, forbidden kind that she suspected Shelburn could give her. She hid a shiver of wicked anticipation at the thought.

When she didn't answer straightaway, Shelburn's soft laugh made every hair on her body bristle in animal response. "You're welcome to second thoughts. You don't have to do anything you don't want to, you know. I'll stand by the terms of our bargain at the Angel. Once we get to Hatfield, I'll see you safe home, if that's your wish."

The problem was that with every minute, Kate's wishes became more improper. At sixteen, she'd been too innocent to do much beyond pine and imagine. Now that she was thirty, the physical presence of the man she wanted sparked all sorts of unprecedented reactions. Once, admiring him from afar had been enough to feed her daydreams. Having that long, splendid body within reach of her greedy hands meant that unrequited yearning no longer satisfied.

"It would almost be easier if you act the villainous seducer," she said, facing him.

When he smiled, attractive creases appeared around his eyes. He'd been a beautiful boy, but by heaven, the man he'd become was magnetically appealing. "I can if you like."

"If you do, I might decide that I need to escape." She should be shocked that he didn't deny his amorous intentions. She worked with men day in, day out, but those professional relationships left her passions untouched. In spite of her inexperience, she could almost see the heat rising in the air between her and Shelburn.

It wasn't altogether a welcome surprise that he found her as compelling as she found him. If he decided to focus all that charm on her seduction, she had no confidence that she could resist him.

And she wasn't yet convinced that she was ready for seduction. Or at least so she told herself.

One dark eyebrow tilted. "Do you want to escape?"

He sounded as if they merely played games. Amusement enriched that already velvety baritone, until it was as intoxicating as rum-soaked currants.

Her hands spread in a baffled gesture. "I should."

The carriage's decorous pace meant that Kate no longer needed to hold on for dear life to keep from falling out. She had a portentous feeling that even if she didn't fall out of the carriage, she verged on falling in a much more significant way. And very soon.

"Ah, 'should.' Such a grim word. I've banished it from my vocabulary."

If even half of what she'd read in the papers was true, he was a man who believed in "would" rather than "should." The exigencies of middle-class morality had no power over the licentious Earl of Shelburn.

When they rounded a bend, the sight of Lord Colville's carriage parked in the center of the road ahead of them saved Kate from having to reply to his last remark.

"I thought they'd be in Hatfield by now," Shelburn muttered, as he slowed his horses to a walk. "What the devil are they doing?"

"They're..." Kate said in shock.

"Kissing. Yes. Well, that's a mercy. It seems they've sorted out their differences at last."

"She was furious with him in Islington."

"She isn't furious with him anymore." Shelburn's expression held no shadows, and he sounded rather jolly when he talked about Lady Verena choosing another man. If he suffered a romantic disappointment, he hid it well. "I'll wager there will be a wedding before the end of May."

The entwined couple should have heard Shelburn's phaeton approaching. But they were too lost in each other to notice anything else. Something powerfully feminine inside Kate twisted, as she observed the unabashed carnality of their kisses. Her blood stirred to a whisper from a world that she'd never entered.

Nobody had ever kissed her like that. In fact, her few experiences with kisses had been brief and rather unpleasant. But Lady Verena and Lord Colville were wrapped tight in each other's arms, and they very near devoured each other in desperation.

Good heavens, was that how Lord Shelburn wanted to kiss her?

A proper lady would be shocked. It seemed she was no proper lady, because that strange, almost painful physical longing inside her coiled tighter, as she imagined Shelburn's mouth exploring hers with such ardor.

Kate told herself to stop thinking about kisses. Instead, she turned to study her companion. "You really don't mind?"

Recent editions of those gossipy papers that she ought to stop reading had been full of hints that Lady Verena and Lord Shelburn were involved. During this season, they'd often been seen in public together.

On the other hand, there hadn't been a hint about Lord Colville courting Lady Verena. In fact, while Lord Colville's political activities often featured in the serious press, he was almost never mentioned in the scandal sheets.

Perhaps Kate shouldn't believe everything that she read. When she'd pored over those sensationalist articles, she'd experienced an utterly pointless pang. She'd loathed the thought of Shelburn marrying another, as if a man of his distinguished lineage would ever consider a common industrialist's daughter as a bride.

"Not a whit." The sultry look he sent her made her toes curl in her half boots. "I have other fish to fry."

Absurd to blush when she was no green girl. "Are you saying I'm an old trout, my lord?"

He burst out laughing. "A beautiful mermaid perhaps."

Shelburn's phaeton rolled up beside the curricle, as Kate struggled to come to terms with the extravagant compliment.

"About time." His tone was mocking.

Colville and Lady Verena didn't spring apart in embarrassment at being caught in a private moment. Instead they straightened with visible reluctance, and regarded Shelburn and Kate as though the interruption emerged from another, faraway world.

Somewhere along the way, Lady Verena had lost her bonnet. Her thick dark hair was tied back with the mannish neckcloth that had once completed the military touches to her traveling dress.

"I see you've caught up at last, Shelburn," Colville said with a coolness that didn't match the glow in his eyes. "You can be the first to congratulate us. Lady Verena has just agreed to marry me."

"It seems she's made her choice." Shelburn's pretense of regret didn't convince Kate. She doubted if it convinced anyone else either. Again, he was being kind to save Lady Verena's pride. He removed his stylish beaver hat and bent his head to the other couple. "I bow to the better man."

"Thank you," Colville said. "I'd offer my condolences, but as you're about to win the race, you'll have my grays. They should provide some consolation."

Shelburn dismissed that suggestion with a careless wave of one gloved hand. "Keep them as an early wedding present. In my view, the race has ended in a draw. Or no, not quite. You've come out the winner in the only way that counts."

More gallantry. Kate studied Shelburn and couldn't help thinking that the rake hadn't completely subsumed the young man who had rescued her sister from social humiliation.

"Perhaps you should introduce us to your companion," Lady Verena said. "I assume that somewhere over the last fifteen miles, you've managed to exchange names."

Shelburn's gaze leveled on Kate with another silent message of sensual interest that set heat rushing through her veins. "Lady Verena Gerard,

Lord Colville. Allow me to present Miss Catherine Starr of Bradbourne in Derbyshire."

Colville bowed. "Miss Starr."

Lady Verena smiled. "Miss Starr."

"My lady. My lord." To her shame, Kate was aware that her smile mightn't be quite so warm, if Shelburn had kept Lady Verena in his sights as a potential lover. "May I add my congratulations into the mix?"

"You may," Verena said.

"Go ahead and claim the victory, my lord," Colville said. "We had a bit of a mishap with the curricle about a mile back. It seems to be in one piece, but I don't want to take too many chances with my precious cargo."

Shelburn frowned, even as he shifted a fraction of an inch closer to Kate on the seat. "What the devil happened?"

He wasn't touching her in any improper way, but she felt that he surrounded her. There was something thrilling about knowing their bodies conducted a secret conversation while a polite discussion continued around them.

"A dog ran out in front of us and almost brought us to grief," Verena said. "No real harm was done."

"Thank the Lord for that," Shelburn said. "Colville, if you can bear to share a carriage, you and I could come in together in my rig and officially make it a draw. That way, the people who placed wagers will get to keep their blunt."

Lady Verena shook her head. "If Eliot arrives at Hatfield as your passenger, people will still say you won, because it's your carriage. I've got a better idea. My cabriolet is following us. With the delays, I imagine it will show up any minute. Why don't you two gentlemen travel in my rig with my horses? Miss Starr and I can follow in Shelburn's phaeton with the grays, and my groom can bring the curricle in last with the chestnuts. I wouldn't leave the grays to him. He's got a good pair of hands, but the horses have had a fright and need careful handling." She glanced at Colville. "That is if you'll trust the grays to me, darling?"

"I trust you with my life. And my horses." The adoration in Lord Colville's smile sparked another of those disturbing twinges in Kate's middle. She couldn't imagine any man ever looking at her like that. Most of all Shelburn. But by heaven, she'd like it if he did.

Lady Verena laughed. "I promise on my soul to take good care of both." She turned to Kate. "What do you think, Miss Starr? I'm a good driver, if you're nervous at all. It's only a couple of miles."

"I'm sure you're more than competent, my lady. I'd be honored to be your passenger."

"That's a capital solution," Shelburn said, even as an unstoppable tide of heat flowed from his body into Kate's. "Given the race has ended with a joyous result but no genuine victor, this should satisfy all parties."

Lord Colville climbed down and said a few words to Lady Verena. Then he looked back. "Your rig is coming up the road right now."

As the cabriolet approached, Lady Verena and Lord Colville went back to murmuring. Declarations of love, Kate guessed.

Kate felt a little awkward, knowing that the two lovers were eager to be alone together. Awkward and mortifyingly relieved. As Hatfield loomed closer, she welcomed the chance to escape Shelburn's distracting presence and try to make sense of her warring impulses. Because once the race was over, she needed to make a decision that would affect the rest of her life. For good or ill.

The day hadn't gone as she'd expected. Not just with this unorthodox ending to the race, but also with Shelburn expressing such swift attraction. It was exhilarating and terrifying in equal amounts.

Kate supposed that because he was a rake, he wasn't fussy about who he bedded. He'd work his wiles on any woman bold enough to accept his invitation back at the Angel.

That reflection didn't please her at all.

"I don't want to let you go," Shelburn said under his breath, as he placed his hand over where hers lay in her lap.

"I'll see you in Hatfield." Despite her trepidation, his admission made Kate's heart expand. "It's not far."

Self-mockery angled his lips down, but a world of desire lay behind his intense stare. "I know." He squeezed her hand. "But it means being parted from you."

"I don't want to leave you either," she admitted in a low voice.

Now that the moment arrived, she wasn't relieved anymore. Instead, superstitious dread stuck its claws into her.

Their meeting was the result of fickle chance. She feared that if she let Shelburn out of her sight, he'd disappear back into the mists of her imagination.

Triumph flared in his eyes. "Damn it, Kate—"

When Colville and Lady Verena turned in their direction, he released her hand and bit off the rest of what he meant to say. Kate appreciated his care for her reputation, but the others must have guessed that she and Shelburn had plans beyond the race.

With a muttered curse that had Kate stifling a laugh, Shelburn climbed down. Straightaway, she missed his nearness.

He began to unharness his chestnuts, demonstrating an impressive competence that told her he didn't rely on his grooms to manage his horses. The possibility of his lordship's competent hands touching her body before too much longer sent another unsettling shiver rippling through her.

Colville helped Lady Verena out of the curricle before leaving her to approach the phaeton. "May I assist you, Miss Starr? Lady Verena has a wonderful touch with the ribbons, you couldn't be in safer hands."

"Thank you," she said, stepping down with his assistance. Close up, Lord Colville was astonishingly handsome. Odd that holding his hand didn't strike even the tiniest spark.

With Verena's groom's help, the new arrangements were soon in place. At a spanking pace, Shelburn and Colville set off for the Greyhound in Lady Verena's cabriolet.

Beside Kate, Lady Verena took up the reins of the phaeton and urged the grays to a more decorous canter. "We should be there in no time, Miss Starr."

Troubled, Kate stared over the horses' backs as her companion steered the carriage with notable skill. Colville hadn't exaggerated when he'd called Lady Verena quite the whip.

What on earth was Kate going to do when they reached Hatfield? When it came to what happened next between them, Shelburn had made it clear that the choice was up to her.

Just what was that choice going to be?

CHAPTER FOUR

"Shelburn missed a treat, when gallantry made him refuse these grays," Lady Verena said, after a few moments of silence while she got the feel of the unfamiliar horses and carriage.

"I know nothing about bloodstock," Kate said. "But they're a handsome pair to look at."

"They are at that. And mouths like velvet. I might have the right to drive them whenever I wish written into the marriage contract. That might frighten Eliot into changing his mind and choosing a more suitable bride."

Kate smiled. "He looks like he's more than happy with his decision, my lady. Right now, I suspect if you demanded his soul on a plate, he'd put a ribbon around it and give it to you."

"And I'm in just as bad a way." Lady Verena's smile held a good deal of self-mockery. "I always swore that I'd never marry again, but it seems love has made a liar of me."

She guided the horses around a sharp turn with a skill that even an ignoramus like Kate could appreciate. The cabriolet was now out of sight.

Colville and Shelburn must already be closing in on Hatfield.

With a straight road ahead, Lady Verena fixed her attention on Kate. While the glow lingered in her fine blue eyes, there was also growing curiosity. "But enough of me, you must tell me about yourself."

Kate shifted in discomfort. Those eyes were dauntingly intelligent, and she felt foolish enough already without exposing her nonsensical motives for taking part in this race. "There's very little to tell."

Lady Verena's mouth quirked. "I don't believe that. The woman who took up Shelburn's scandalous invitation with such impressive sangfroid has a nerve to match my own."

Kate wasn't prepared to confide in someone who was little more than a stranger, however charming she might be. "As his lordship said, it will be a tale to tell my grandchildren." If she ever got around to having children who could then give her grandchildren. The way her life tended, there was no guarantee that she would. "Everyone needs a small adventure now and again."

Lady Verena's laugh held a hint of appreciation. "You're determined to remain an enigma, I can see. But it's obvious that you're a respectable woman. I suspect that nobody was more surprised than Shelburn when you took him up on his challenge and joined him in the phaeton."

"If you're talking about shock, my cousins weren't far behind him."

"They were the people with you at the inn?"

"Yes." Her cousins had lived with her the last ten years. Hazel had proven a diligent chaperone, sometimes too diligent, and Alfred helped to manage the mills, although Kate sometimes had to stop him claiming an authority that neither his marriage to her cousin nor his abilities justified.

"Anyway, I take my hat off to you. Or I would, if I hadn't lost it in that pestilential carriage mishap. I've never been one to think women should be meek and mild. I like a lady with a bit of backbone. You, Miss Starr, are definitely that. When you get back to London, will you call on me?"

Troubled, Kate studied this lovely, generous creature. "I don't think that would be suitable."

Verena stiffened, and a hint of hauteur entered her tone. "I beg your pardon. For a moment, I forgot the scandals attached to my name."

Kate regarded her companion in horror. "That's not at all what I meant, my lady. Forgive me if I caused offense." She made an apologetic gesture with one gloved hand. "You're a duke's daughter, and you're about to wed a man who will inherit an earldom. We don't move in the same circles. A woman who runs the family business is well below your notice."

Verena's expression remained somber. "You seem very well-informed for someone who claims no interest in the beau monde."

"I never said I wasn't interested." Kate felt her cheeks heat. "I have a lamentable weakness for high society gossip. But that doesn't mean I belong in your world."

"Yet you accepted Shelburn's invitation – and if you read the scandal sheets, you must know all about his reputation."

And mine. Although unspoken, Kate heard the last words in her mind.

"I know who he is."

"So this was a chance for a brief visit to a realm you'd only imagined?"

Lady Verena had no idea how close she veered to the truth. "If you like," Kate said soberly. "But that doesn't turn me into a highborn lady."

Verena shrugged. "I think you're intriguing. And so does Shelburn. I've known him since I was a girl, and I recognize the signs of interest. If you're open to a flirtation, he'd be more than willing."

By flirtation, Kate was well aware that Lady Verena meant an affair. "All I accepted was a carriage ride."

Lady Verena raised an eyebrow. "Was it?"

No, it wasn't. Kate avoided the question. "I'd love to call on you, if you wouldn't feel I was being pushy. But I fear I'm too pragmatic and tradesman-like to be your friend."

Verena's laugh had regained its warmth. "You'll make a nice change from my other acquaintances, then."

Kate exhaled in relief. It seemed her gaffe was forgiven. "Then if you don't mind hearing about the manufacture of cotton, I look forward to visiting."

Lady Verena cast her an unimpressed glance. "Oh, I'm sure we'll find plenty of other things to talk about. Don't imagine you've diverted me from my questions. I sense a mystery here, and I'm terrible when I want to know a thing."

Kate's laugh wasn't quite so easy as Lady Verena's. "You're going to be too busy planning a wedding to worry about anything else."

"And Eliot will want to take me somewhere extravagant for our honeymoon. I can already tell."

"Poor you," Kate said with ironic sympathy.

Lady Verena laughed again. "I don't know how I'll bear it. The promise of bliss will be... Goodness me, what is he up to?"

Kate had been looking at Lady Verena rather than the road ahead, so it was a surprise to glance up and see an unfamiliar gig heading toward them.

"Shelburn, what on earth are you doing here? Don't you trust me to deliver your Miss Starr safe into your clutches?"

The carriage might be unfamiliar, but the driver wasn't. Nor was the zing of awareness that had Kate sitting up straight as he came alongside.

He swept off his hat and bowed to the two ladies. "Verena. Miss Starr. It turns out the Greyhound is heaving with people who came out yesterday to see the end of the race. I thought I'd save Miss Starr all that curiosity."

More kindness. "Thank you. I can't imagine anyone there will know me, but I'd rather not take the chance."

"Very gallant," Lady Verena said in a dry tone, although it *was* in fact very gallant. "Were you greeted with howls of disappointment when you and Eliot arrived together without declaring a winner?"

"Tearing of hair and gnashing of teeth, my dear."

Lady Verena laughed. "I can imagine. I expect that the shock when Eliot and I announce our engagement will make up for the letdown."

"Those fribbles love to be in on the news first. The Edgecombes are there. Once Celia hears, Eliot won't need to place a notice in the *Morning Post*."

Lady Verena turned to Kate. "Miss Starr, are you happy to travel on with this reprobate? I can drive you where you'd like to go, if not."

Verena's perceptive gaze told Kate that her new friend already saw much more than she'd admitted to. Her new friend was also notably gracious to offer to delay her reunion with the man she loved.

Kate nodded. "Yes, I'll go with his lordship. But thank you."

"I hope we meet again."

Kate smiled. "So do I."

She climbed down from the phaeton and crossed to take Shelburn's hand, so he could help her into the gig. Once again, that immediate thrill of contact made her stomach feel all strange and quivery.

Lady Verena touched the handle of her whip to her forehead. "Godspeed, Shelburn."

"And to you as well, Verena. There's a gentleman waiting at the Greyhound who isn't showing the patience of a...*saint*."

Lady Verena smiled at Shelburn's sly reference to Colville's not altogether kind nickname. "Oh, Eliot isn't half the saint you might think. If he was, he wouldn't have anything to do with a miserable sinner like me."

It was Shelburn's turn to laugh. "Never miserable, Verena. In fact, I'm sure the two of you are going to be disgustingly happy together."

Verena's smile conveyed such joy that Kate looked away. It was clear that the lady loved and was loved in return. What a marvelous feeling that must be.

It was petty to feel envious. But envious she was.

"I'm sure we will be, too," Verena responded with a laugh. "And now I must go because—"

"Because you want to be with Colville."

"I do." She sighed. "Eliot and I have wasted too much time on things that don't matter. I hope you'll take a lesson from that."

Before Shelburn could reply to that piece of unsolicited advice, Lady Verena urged the grays to a swift trot and drove away in Hatfield's direction.

Kate was never shy. She'd been running the mills since she was twenty and before that, she'd helped her father. She was more accustomed to masculine company than gossiping with female friends.

But as she watched Lady Verena disappear down the road, she felt awkward and unprepared and...shy. Unseeing, she stared down at the hands that she'd linked in her lap to hide their shaking.

"Would you like to go back to London?" For once, Shelburn's voice held no sardonic humor. Instead he sounded gentle. Which didn't help resolve her clamoring confusion.

Back to London? If she left him, she'd be safe. She could pursue her sensible plans. After all, she'd spent her life being sensible.

She lifted her head and turned to study the man beside her. He was handsome and wild and dashing, and entirely outside her experience. Nobody who knew her would ever believe that staid Kate Starr gave the time of day to such an aristocratic libertine.

She had difficulty believing it herself, despite all the foolish dreams that she'd woven about him.

But when she'd permitted herself those foolish dreams, she'd been sure that Lord Shelburn would forever remain a figure of fantasy. She'd never have to deal with the real man.

Until she did.

Now it was up to her to bring this escapade to a close. Hazel would reproach her. Alfred would sniff with disapproval. Mr. Williams would overlook her small misdeed, she was sure. And if he couldn't, her life would toddle on with no ill effects.

Should she pass up the business opportunity that Mr. Williams offered, she'd find another. Or continue along as she was, which would be no bad thing.

Going back to London was the correct choice. The *sensible* choice.

How she began to loathe that word "sensible."

Shelburn remained quiet. She suspected that he was wise enough to recognize that if she could blame him for any lapse in her judgment, she would. He wasn't giving her the chance. This was a decision she had to make. She needed to accept that if there were consequences, they were of her own making.

"Where would you like to take me?"

The clumsy question made her blush like fire. Because she was sure that if she agreed to run off with Shelburn, he would indeed end up taking her.

The light flaring in his eyes told her that he hadn't missed her slip. Although his voice remained grave when he replied. "There's a good inn I sometimes use about five miles away."

Sometimes used for an encounter with a mistress? What else could he mean? Kate had no illusions about this man's appetite for a new woman in his bed. "And what do you want of me at this good inn?"

He didn't look away. But then, settling the terms for an affair was nothing new for him. She supposed she should be grateful that he didn't take her consent for granted. Someone as experienced as Shelburn must know that she was attracted to him. She was too unfamiliar with desire to hide it.

"I think you already know."

She shifted on the seat of the hired carriage. It was roomier than the phaeton. So it made no sense that she was even more conscious of his proximity than she had been on the drive north from the Angel. "Tell me anyway. I can't afford to misunderstand what is happening."

He set the horses moving at an easy walk. They were nothing like the thoroughbreds that he'd driven up from London. They were more like the reliable, commonplace beasts that Kate kept in her stables. She had a grim feeling that there was a lesson in that for her. Shelburn was the high-strung, expensive champion, while Kate was the plodding workhorse.

She pushed the thought aside as too depressing for words.

"I don't want the horses standing," he said, clearly thinking that she misinterpreted his action as an attempt to force her hand. "I'm not kidnapping you."

"I almost wish you would," she said in a shaky voice that she didn't recognize as her own.

He cast her a piercing glance under the brim of that stylish hat. "No, you don't."

No, she didn't. She'd battled all her life to retain the right to make her own decisions. Even in today's unprecedented circumstances, she wouldn't give that independence up without a fight.

She swallowed to moisten a throat dry with nerves and straightened her spine against the padded leather seat. "So tell me."

The horses proceeded so slowly that Shelburn could devote his attention to her, while keeping a loose hold on the reins. "I want you."

His words filled her with wicked pleasure. Kate struggled to keep a grip on caution, but excitement vibrated in her voice when she spoke. "Because I'm a woman who happened to drive with you to Hatfield?"

"We didn't make it to Hatfield."

She didn't smile. "You know what I mean."

"I was trying to lighten the atmosphere." A faint smile teased that expressive mouth. "I feel a little as if I'm going to the scaffold, instead of plotting a secret rendezvous."

Kate stiffened. "That's not very flattering."

His laugh held an ironic note. "Perhaps not."

"I'm not...I'm not accustomed to dalliance."

He sighed and returned his attention to the ambling horses. "No, I see that."

Unfortunately, he was right about the intense atmosphere. She couldn't blame him for feeling oppressed.

When she didn't speak, he went on. "I want you because you dared to join me on this ride. I want you because from the moment I saw you across that crowded innyard, I felt like you and I were meant to come together. I'm known for being outrageous, and luring a respectable lady to join me in my carriage was indeed outrageous. But I didn't invite you to amuse the numbskulls who spread society tattle. I invited you because I had the strangest feeling that if I let you go on your way, I'd miss out on an experience unsurpassed even in my unruly life." While she struggled to digest his confession – and it sounded like a confession that he didn't much enjoy making – he went on. "And of course, I want you because you're beautiful."

"That's very nice of you to say." She'd barely stopped blushing since she'd mentioned him taking her. Now she blushed again. "I'm a little too severe and mannish for the current fashion."

"That's not at all how I'd describe you, you know." This time, he gave her a real smile, as he subjected her to a thorough inspection that left her feeling as if she may as well not be wearing this modest traveling outfit. It was apparent that this man knew everything about a woman's body.

Her breasts swelled against her pelisse's dark blue bodice as if they begged for his touch. Her heart raced. Not just because he made her feel naked. The avid interest in his expression had her pulses performing a wild tarantella.

There was no doubt that Lord Shelburn was an exciting man. The problem was that Kate was convinced that she wasn't an exciting woman.

If she did this reckless, dangerous thing, was she doomed to disappoint him? She had enough pride to want him to enjoy what they did together. If she set out to fall in such a spectacular fashion, she wanted the occasion to be memorable for him, too.

She shifted on the seat again, in part to ease a stomach churning with nerves and wanton excitement. "How would you describe me?"

His smile turned tender. She wished it wouldn't. When he looked at her like that, he had far too much power over her. "Are you chasing compliments?"

"I think I am." With difficulty, she unlinked her shaking hands and made a bewildered gesture. "It might stiffen my resolution."

He gave a grunt of amusement. "Whereas my resolution is quite stiff enough already."

More blushes. She was worldly enough to understand the joke. "So?"

He pulled the horses to a halt and waited for a farm cart to pass. He touched his hat in salute to the family riding on it, all in their Sunday best and on their way back from church, Kate guessed. It was hard to believe that it wasn't even noon yet. She felt like her whole life had changed today. A mere few hours did no justice to the turmoil she'd experienced.

"So you're beautiful. All woman. Tall and graceful and mysterious. Like a goddess come down to earth. Minerva or Juno. Someone glorious and powerful. If you don't already know that, I have no respect at all for the clodpolls who live in Bradbourne. They should be falling at your feet in worship whenever they catch a glimpse of you."

That did make her laugh, even as astonishment ripped through her. Shelburn seemed to be talking about some other person entirely.

Kate was no self-effacing mouse. She was well aware of her qualities, even if most of them fell under the category of sturdy and useful rather than alluring. She was clever and hardworking and determined. She was loyal to a fault – look at how her foolish heart had settled on Lord Shelburn and had never shifted. But none of those qualities conveyed the touch of the divine that he claimed to see in her.

"That would be devilish inconvenient." Because it was so ridiculous to think of practical, businesslike Kate Starr as a resident of Olympus, she had no trouble injecting a dry note into her answer. "And dangerous as well, if it happened in the mill with the machines running."

Shelburn burst out laughing. "You're enchanting, you know."

"No, I don't," she said crisply. "So you can keep your nonsense to yourself, my lord."

He urged the horses on again, at that same leisured pace. "It doesn't feel like nonsense to want a woman the way I want you." His gaze sharpened. "What's it to be, Kate? Do I turn off at the next corner? Or shall we retrace our way to the Angel? If we turn off the main road, I'll take you to my bed and show you pleasure beyond your wildest dreams."

His intent dark gaze made her blood accelerate into a hot torrent. She noticed that he'd stopped calling her Miss Starr. The sound of her name on his lips thrilled her. It promised more intimacies to come.

"That won't be difficult." She swallowed again to ease a throat tight with nerves. "I've never known pleasure."

He understood straightaway what she was saying. Kate saw it in his face. She read surprise there and unexpected satisfaction. "My already fading respect for the men of Bradbourne has disappeared altogether."

"I think I rather terrify them. I'm quite hardheaded when it comes to business."

"What a bunch of cowards. None of them are worthy of you. You're no fool. That's appealing rather than off-putting."

A huff of wry laughter escaped her. "But then we're not in the middle of negotiations."

He didn't smile back. "Aren't we?"

She supposed that they were. "If we are, I'm not feeling very hardheaded."

"Nor am I."

She didn't believe him. Shelburn must have completed these preliminaries to an affair a thousand times. He was trying to make her feel special. Which could be kindness, or could be a rake's strategy for obtaining a skittish lady's cooperation.

Although Kate suspected that most of the ladies he set his sights on were considerably more used to flirtations than she was. She made herself put aside the thorny thought of those other ladies. And the multitudes more who would no doubt follow her into his arms.

If she was going to do this, she refused to succumb to romantic dreams of Shelburn falling in love with her. Love wasn't part of the arrangement. She'd caught his interest for the moment. That was more than she'd ever imagined she'd do.

The question was whether the chance of a short liaison with the man she'd always wanted outweighed the plans she'd made for the rest of her life.

In general, she was a strategic thinker. Sacrificing long-term gain for current reward wasn't her way. It was one of the reasons that she'd managed to survive and thrive in business, despite the forces ranged against a lone woman running a successful enterprise.

"The turn to the inn is coming up. What would you like to do?"

Kate should appreciate Lord Shelburn's willingness to leave the choice to her. A pity that she didn't. She looked around the empty fields surrounding them and thought about her past. And the future that she'd accepted, at least until this morning.

Not to mention the future that awaited, if she did this outlandish thing.

Although she supposed that was no great mystery. She imagined that once she and Shelburn parted, she'd return to running the mill, managing her workforce, living day to day with nothing but profits to show for her efforts. That was how her father had taught her to proceed.

Perhaps it was time that she looked for a fulfillment beyond the financial. And this opportunity would never come again.

Kate was surprised at how steady her voice was when she replied. "Take me to the inn, my lord."

CHAPTER FIVE

ost in delight, Shelburn regarded this astonishing creature. She'd crossed his path with no warning, but she enthralled him as no woman had in years. Perhaps ever.

This morning, heaven had smiled on him. Perhaps it was a reward for his good deed in helping Verena to make it up with her beloved. Although given how short his list of good deeds was compared with all his sins, he doubted that was the case.

"My lord?" Kate asked when he didn't speak.

She sounded composed. She'd sounded composed the whole time that he'd known her, although he wasn't fool enough to imagine she took any of this lightly.

He'd be the first to admit that life had spoiled him. A large fortune. Luck when it came to women and the gaming tables.

It would be churlish to find all this good fortune a tad boring. But the sad truth was that with so many good things falling into his lap, he couldn't help feeling a little jaded. Without doubt, he was bored with the obvious. The women who angled for his attention were all so damned easy to pluck.

No suspense. No chase. Nothing at stake. No real satisfaction in the victory.

In fact, where was the victory, when they were so eager to fling themselves at his head?

Who could blame him for taking advantage of his opportunities? Well, it was true that many of the sticklers did. Even called him the worst lord in London. Which mightn't be altogether fair – there were plenty of scoundrels who could compete for that honor. But it was close enough to fair to have stuck.

Perhaps the brazen nature of his transgressions got up his critics' noses. Perhaps it was that no love affair ever left a mark. If there was one thing the world's moral guardians abhorred, it was a man who walked the primrose path to emerge unscathed and smiling at his destination.

Even after a few hours in her company – and not particularly revealing hours at that – he could tell that Kate Starr was his complete opposite in every way. He didn't give a rat's arse if the world knew his business. She was reticent to the point of secretiveness. He'd always been shallow. She had depths that lured a man to want to drown in them.

One thing that they did share was a bone-deep self-confidence. But while she might rely on strength of character, he was a wayward gentleman who knew that charm, noble birth, and a liberal application of cash would get him out of any scrape. And if those three remedies should fail, he could always fall back on sheer bloody impudence.

How daunting to suspect that none of those qualities impressed Miss Starr.

Yet something must have. She'd agreed to come to the Merry Haymaker with him. He didn't pretend to understand it. A woman this magnificent should despise him as a useless wastrel.

Shelburn knew better than to tangle with respectable virgins. And good Lord, Kate must be at least thirty, so she'd held onto her virtue way past the point where most women chose a lover or a husband. Not through lack of options, he was sure. However self-deprecating she was about her attractions, he'd wager a fortune that he wasn't the only man who had burned to ruffle that endless tranquility.

When he'd bedded all those wild widows and bored wives and avaricious ballet dancers, he knew just where he stood with them. No surprises lurked under the sheets. His affairs were almost as businesslike as he imagined Miss Starr was with her customers.

He always enjoyed a good tussle on a mattress. Damn it, he wasn't unnatural. It was just that the significance of what he did never seemed to stretch much past a moment's pleasure.

"My lord, shall we go?"

Shelburn realized that he was gawping at her like a yokel newly come to London. He gave his head a quick shake to straighten thoughts in utter disarray. It didn't help.

Only when he blinked to banish distraction did he realize that the carriage remained stationary in the middle of the road. Thank goodness, it was Sunday and there wasn't much traffic, or he might pose a dangerous hazard.

By Jove, Kate Starr was a dangerous hazard, despite that calm manner and modest demeanor. Shelburn had a growing feeling that she had the capacity to bring him crashing down in ruins.

Which didn't mean he intended to let her get away.

"Yes." He gathered up the reins and reminded himself that he was a famous whip. He knew how to handle a carriage and horses. "Yes, right now."

Damn it, he knew how to handle a woman, too. No female had put him in quite such a fluster since…

Since forever.

Even his first lovers had fallen into his arms without difficulty.

So, he realized, had Miss Starr. Odd that despite this, gaining her consent made him feel like he'd won a great prize.

He flicked the reins and urged the lazy nags to a trot, as he guided the gig onto the correct side of the road. What the devil was wrong with him today? He was acting like a raw boy with his first sweetheart. And despite his enormous experience with the fair sex, he'd never had something as innocent as a sweetheart. All far too romantic for the wicked Earl of Shelburn.

"I thought for a moment that you might have changed your mind," Kate said in a thready voice.

He'd come back to himself enough to laugh, as the hired horses broke into a canter. At this moment, he had more incentive to speed than he'd ever had during the race with Colville.

"Never."

In record time, they covered the distance to the inn on the outskirts of the neat village of Walford. Kate had retreated back into silence. She really was a sphinx. A beautiful sphinx.

Shelburn was used to women who talked and giggled and fussed and teased. It turned out to be dashed peaceful to sit beside a woman who was content to keep her thoughts to herself.

Or at least so he believed, until curiosity began to gnaw at him.

By God, he couldn't remember the last time that he'd been curious about a woman's thoughts. Kate was such an enigma that he hungered to discover what went on inside her head.

Would she remain a mystery, once he'd used her body?

His cynical side insisted that Kate Starr would turn out to be like every other woman he'd seduced. Entertaining in the short term, then eminently forgettable.

But some deeper instinct warned Shelburn that for once he wouldn't get everything his own way. So far, Kate was engaging and interesting and unusual. That instinct predicted that she promised to become more rather than less fascinating as he unraveled her secrets.

When the carriage clattered into the empty innyard, two grooms rushed out to hold his horses. The landlord bustled through the door, followed by his rotund wife. "My lord, we weren't expecting you. But welcome, welcome. Your usual rooms are available, if you're thinking of staying."

"Good day, Fletcher. I was in the area and thought I'd call in for luncheon."

"Very good, sir." The landlord bowed. "Mrs. Fletcher has a leg of lamb in the oven that will bring tears to your eyes."

"I remember the last one I had here. Good enough for the Prince Regent's table."

"You *are* a regular guest," Kate said in an undertone from beside him.

Since his boyhood, he hadn't felt an ounce of shame for anything that he'd done. Now he hid a wince. "It's convenient and near enough to London. And the food is good."

And the beds were large and soft, and the sheets were clean, and his lavish tips ensured the staff's discretion and prompt attention.

Kate wasn't the first woman he'd brought here. Not by a long mark. All of a sudden, that seemed wrong. Because whatever happened between them, she deserved better than his usual carelessness. He didn't want to treat her like just another bored lady of the ton, keen to learn whether the worst lord in London was the excellent lover he was purported to be.

"I'm sure the dining room is worth the detour," she said with more of the subtle mockery that shouldn't sting, but somehow did.

"My lord, is there any luggage?" one of the grooms asked.

"No, not today, Fred," Shelburn said with a nonchalance that for once wasn't completely natural.

The man bowed. "Very good, sir."

He and his colleague retreated to a respectful distance, as it became clear that Shelburn wasn't yet ready to step down from the carriage.

"I should take you somewhere else," Shelburn muttered. "By Jupiter, if I had an ounce of conscience, I should take you back to London. You're too fine for a furtive affair with a blackguard like me."

Kate regarded him in horror. "Don't you dare develop scruples at this juncture, Shelburn."

"I know it's not like me—"

"If I've steeled my nerves to give myself to a rake, the rake can damn well steel himself to do the deed." Her tone was crisp and purposeful.

Amazed, he studied the remarkable face beneath the stylish bonnet. "Scruples and I have been strangers since I was in the nursery."

Her lips tightened. In amusement or disapproval? He wasn't sure. What he was sure about was his craving to discover if she tasted as pure and fresh as spring water.

"There's no need to sound so proud of the fact."

His laugh held a hint of chagrin. "I don't want to do wrong by you."

When she met his eyes, at last he perceived the heat simmering in those green-brown depths. It turned out that her surface coolness had been deceptive. "Yet here I am, hoping you're about to ruin me."

He sighed. His better self, so often absent, had tried to dissuade him from bedding her. But if she was so deuced fired up to lose her maidenhead, he was ready to consign his better self to Hades. "How can I say no?"

Her dark eyebrows arched. "Why on earth would you?"

Some distant corner of his mind told him that he needed to think further before he proceeded. If only to convince Kate that there was more to him than a rapacious debaucher, who fell on any available woman the way he feared he was about to fall on Mrs. Fletcher's roast lamb. But rising desire overwhelmed that faint whisper of caution.

"Are you hungry?"

She knew that he didn't just mean for food, although she must be famished as well. "Starving."

Need slammed through him, and every sense went on bristling alert. She might be inexperienced, but she wasn't unaware. And whatever her reasons, it was evident that she wanted him, too.

Shelburn sent Kate a quick smile before glancing toward their audience, who awaited his convenience. "We'll stay for luncheon, Fletcher."

"And the rooms, my lord?"

"We'll take those as well." As Fred returned to hold the horses, Shelburn descended from the gig and walked around to help Kate to alight. Every time he touched her, heat sparked in his blood. By the time he got her to himself, he feared that he'd be a complete wreck.

"Thank you, my lord," she said coolly, as if she spent her life visiting country inns with dalliance in mind.

By God, she was game. She might describe herself as staid and modest, but he could see that she possessed an effrontery to match his own.

"Allow me to show you upstairs, my lord and lady," Mrs. Fletcher said. "I'll have hot water sent up, so you can wash off the travel dust before dining."

Keeping hold of Kate's hand, Shelburn preceded the innkeeper's wife into the building. "Thank you."

After the bright light outside, the inn's interior was dark, and to his relief empty of everyone but the Fletchers. He'd avoided Hatfield because he wanted to save Kate from an avalanche of speculation. It would be a pity if they encountered nosy onlookers here at Walford. "You're not busy at the moment?"

"Not today, no." Mrs. Fletcher took the lead and started to climb the stairs. "But last night, we didn't have a bed to spare, and gentlemen slept in the taproom and the downstairs parlor. Your race with Lord Colville brought so many people out from London that Hatfield was packed to the rafters. We got the overflow."

"I hope you won, my lord," Fletcher said from below them.

"I won in every way that matters," he muttered to Kate, which made her smile at him with an approval that he liked far too much. From the landing, he glanced down at Fletcher. "It was a draw, which means all those London flibbertigibbets wasted a trip."

"Aye, well, they don't have anything better to do, I suppose."

Mrs. Fletcher brought them along a short corridor and opened the door to the familiar sitting room with views over the blossoming orchards at the back of the inn. "Would you like your meal served here, my lord? The best private parlor is free if you'd rather eat downstairs."

"Here, thank you, Mrs. Fletcher." He took off his gloves and hat and placed both on a side table. He passed his driving coat to Mrs. Fletcher, so she could take it away for a good brushing.

"Very good, sir. Dinner will be about half an hour, if that's convenient."

Shelburn glanced at Kate who gave a small nod. She tugged off her gloves, revealing two white, graceful hands. The thought of those elegant hands exploring his body crashed through him like a blow from a bare-knuckle fighter.

Her continued silence hinted at discomfort with being under a stranger's observation, he thought. He was learning to read her. She was a complex woman, and one needed to look beneath the surface to understand what was going on.

"Yes, that's fine. Please send up a bottle of that fine claret I had last time and perhaps some barley water, too." His throat was dry. He imagined Kate felt the same. "And see if Fletcher can dig out some shaving tackle for me."

Shelburn had shaved before leaving home this morning, but that was hours ago. He didn't want his bristles to chafe Kate's fine skin. On his previous visits to the Merry Haymaker, he'd arrived with luggage and his valet and all the necessities of life.

"The local barber is in the taproom, sir. Shall I send him up?"

"Capital."

Mrs. Fletcher curtsied, as Kate took off her bonnet and wandered across to the diamond-paned windows opening onto the fine spring day. If Mrs. Fletcher said anything more before she left, Shelburn didn't hear it. He was too busy staring transfixed at his latest mistress.

Her bonnet had concealed a wealth of rich brown hair that combined every shade of autumn. Russet and gold and bronze. His hands curled at his sides, as he imagined unpinning that luxuriant mass and seeing it ripple around those straight shoulders.

Vaguely he heard the door shut. "May I take your coat?"

Kate turned to give him a small smile. "Yes, please."

He stepped behind her and sucked in a lungful of her scent, familiar after their travel. A hint of dust and perspiration. Flowers. Something warm and evocative that was hers alone.

Under the upswept coiffure, strands of silky mahogany hair clung to her nape. To his surprise, his hands were unsteady as he brushed the tendrils out of the way. Dear Lord, no woman had ever made him shake. Except this one.

She started under his touch and released a soft huff of breath that didn't sound like a protest. The fleeting contact thundered through him. It was the first time that they'd met skin to skin.

Shelburn lifted his hands off her, while he waited for Kate to undo the line of buttons down the front of her coat. Then unable to resist, he caught her shoulders and kissed the pale neck rising long and slender beneath the piles of dusky hair. For the first time, he tasted the warmth of her skin.

She tensed for an instant, before he felt her loosen. "Oh…"

Her scent was potent here. He felt her tremble under his lips.

Shelburn had to force himself to raise his head, so he could draw the coat away. Without looking, he tossed it across to the armchair near the unlit fireplace. Then he couldn't resist kissing her nape again.

She made a husky little sound of encouragement and angled back in a silent but unmistakable plea for more. How could he resist? He slid his arms around her waist and pulled her against his body.

He was already hard. When his hips jutted forward into that luscious rump, she'd know how excited he was.

Kissing the satiny skin at the side of her neck, he lingered on the sensitive nerves beneath her ear. She shivered, and her gasp communicated surprise as well as enjoyment. As he firmed his hold, she pressed closer.

"That's wicked," she sighed, tilting her head to give him better access. "It makes me feel all…shaky and unsteady."

"Good." Feeling rather shaky and unsteady himself, he smiled against her skin. He kissed her again, avid to hear more of those breathy sounds of pleasure, and slid his hands up to cup her voluptuous bosom.

"Shelburn…"

When he shaped his hands to those luscious swells of flesh, he heard her breath hitch. Then with an abruptness that left him at a loss, she straightened and pulled away.

He frowned. Everything he knew about women – far too much for the good of his soul – told him that she'd liked what he'd done. So why the devil did she stop? "Kate?"

Frustration tinged her low laugh. He realized why when Mrs. Fletcher and a maid marched in, carrying canisters of steaming water.

They must have knocked. They did most of the time. But he'd been so lost in the preliminaries to seduction that he'd heard nothing past the blood pounding in his ears and Kate's ravishing sighs.

He shouldn't be embarrassed. The Fletchers knew what he'd come to the inn to do. For heaven's sake, he and his companion had turned up without prior arrangements and without luggage.

Even if there was any question about Shelburn's intentions, Kate looked charmingly guilty. Pink tinged her cheeks and with her tousled hair and bright eyes, it was obvious that she'd just been in his arms.

Once again, he wished he could take her somewhere untarnished by a past that right now smacked of the tawdry. But all his properties were well south of Hertfordshire, in Dorset and Devon. With warning, he could have arranged to use a friend's house. But even if he could bear to delay the affair, he feared that Kate might change her mind if given too long to contemplate her fall from grace.

Shelburn turned away and struggled for control. He was all kinds of an impetuous idiot. What the hell had he been thinking? He knew that he and Kate had no privacy. At least until they'd dined and the plates had been cleared away. Yet he was an inch from pitching pleasant, polite Mrs. Fletcher and her minions out the window.

By heaven, it wasn't even midday yet. He prided himself on being a civilized man and a considerate lover, yet he was so mad for Kate, he was ready to tumble her without an ounce of ceremony.

Her nearness sent every thought flying, except for his need for her. The taste of her skin lingered on his lips. His hands still curled to fit the shape of her breasts.

"Shall I put the water in the dressing room, my lord?"

He didn't turn around. In these tight breeches, his arousal must be all too visible.

"My lady will use the bedroom." His answer sounded scratchy. "I'll use the dressing room."

"Very good, sir. Franny, you take that can in for his lordship." Mrs. Fletcher opened the door to the bedroom and went through to fill the large earthenware ewer on the washstand.

Shelburn noticed that Kate's attention fixed on the bedroom. He hoped like blazes that the sight of the huge four-poster didn't snap her out of her recklessness.

A short, plump fellow with pomaded hair appeared at the door with a leather bag in his hand. "My lord, you requested a shave?"

Shelburn bit back a savage curse at yet another interruption, even if it was one that he'd asked for. By now, he'd gained sufficient control of himself to face the new arrival. "Yes, please. Shall we go into the dressing room?"

"Very good, my lord."

Shelburn dared to meet Kate's eyes. She no longer looked quite so dazed. Instead her face was alight with amusement. He'd feared that she might be mortified to be caught mid-clinch, but not for the first time, he commended her sangfroid.

He recognized that practicalities were going to rule for the immediate future, blast it all. "Shall I see you back here when our meal is served?"

"I'd be delighted," she said in a steady voice – although both of them knew that the real delight would only come once they were alone together.

CHAPTER SIX

By the time Shelburn sat down to an excellent meal in the attractive sitting room, he was in a better frame of mind. He'd washed, and he'd had a decent shave. A fire now blazed in the hearth. It was all enough to remind him that he was a gentleman with at least a shred of self-control.

Kate and he had the rest of the day together to explore the attraction flaring between them. He could wait until they were safe from interruptions before he slaked his passions.

That resolution took a hit when Kate appeared from the bedroom. The blue traveling dress under her concealing coat turned out to be fashionable and stylish – and even better, if not for his good intentions, it revealed a tempting amount of her statuesque figure.

Earlier, he'd been in such a state that he hadn't dared to take in too many details of Kate's appearance. He knew the limits of his restraint.

She'd rearranged her hair, too, in soft waves that made his fingers itch to let it down.

Soon, he told himself. Soon.

In the meantime, he meant to find out more about her. Physical pleasure beckoned, but so did the chance to feed his curiosity about his bewitching companion.

He pulled out a chair for her. "Mrs. Fletcher must have known we were hungry."

Kate smiled with appreciation at the feast set out before them. She sat down and picked up her napkin. "It smells wonderful."

"Would you like some wine? Fletcher keeps a good cellar. It's one of the reasons I'm a regular customer."

Not the main reason, as both he and Kate were aware. "Yes, please."

Shelburn wasn't a man who tolerated jealousy in his lovers. To his shame, he never cared enough about the women he bedded to be jealous. The moment a mistress threw a tantrum about his interest in someone else, the affair ended.

Only now did he think that was a cursed cold-blooded way to carry on. Perhaps his point of view had changed since seeing Verena fall so deeply in love with Colville. Not long ago, Shelburn would have wagered a substantial sum on his capricious childhood friend being incapable of the emotion. Perhaps self-knowledge knocked at his door, because even at this early stage, he felt an affinity with Kate that promised to prove more profound than his most torrid love affair.

He mightn't believe in jealousy, but he already knew that he wouldn't like Kate to turn to another man. Even worse, he wanted her to be jealous of his other amours. It might be another unflattering reflection on his character, but he preferred to have every ounce of her attention fixed on him.

Shelburn poured the wine and took his place across the table. "May I serve you?"

"Yes, thank you." Then she gave a laugh of such astonishing dirtiness that he almost forgot his good intentions and leaped across to seize her in his arms. "Why is it that everything we say has a double meaning? You're proving disastrous to my good character, my lord."

"I do so hope that's the case," he purred.

"I'm sure you do." She passed a plate across. "But I fear how I'll fit back into my productive, blameless life after all this sin."

He refused to think of the end of their affair before it even started. Although Kate seemed to suffer no qualms about contemplating her departure, damn it. "You should call me Leighton."

"Very well."

He filled her plate with roast lamb and baked vegetables and poured Mrs. Fletcher's excellent wine gravy over the meat. "Enough?"

"Yes, thank you. I'm afraid you're about to discover that I eat like a starving navvy. You must be used to fine ladies who nibble half a sugar wafer before proclaiming themselves unable to manage another bite."

"I like a woman with a zest for life's pleasures." He slid her loaded plate in front of her then began to serve himself. "And before you ask, I don't just mean food."

"I didn't think you did," she said with more of that intriguing calmness. A man could spend a lifetime with someone like this and relish the lack of theatrics.

Shelburn's mistresses were always prone to theatrics. Until he'd met Kate, he hadn't realized how restful serenity and good sense could be. Probably because he'd had so little experience of either.

His mother and sisters were lovable but incapable of managing without a man's guidance. Kate Starr, he was sure, could run the country and still have time to spare.

He set his plate down and raised his full glass. "Shall I make a toast?"

"To life's pleasures?"

"If you prefer."

"Then, yes." She raised her glass, too. "Also I'd like to wish your friends Lady Verena and Lord Colville many happy years together."

"Well said." He waved his glass then sipped the wine, without shifting his gaze from hers. She had beautiful eyes, such a mixture of shades. It was difficult to say if they were green or gold.

Shelburn waited until she'd eaten most of her meal before he reminded her of her promise. The bottle of wine was half-empty, and he hadn't missed the surreptitious glances she cast him under her thick sable lashes. Like him, she became impatient with the delay.

"You said that when we got to Hatfield, you'd explain why you came with me," he said softly.

Her lips firmed. With a purposeful movement, she placed her knife and fork together on the plate. "As you pointed out, we didn't make it to Hatfield."

"You won't tell me?"

He caught her hand in the middle of a bewildered gesture. She gasped at the contact, then curled her fingers around his as he lowered her hand to rest on the tablecloth.

"I'll sound like a fool."

For pity's sake, he hadn't got a thrill from holding a woman's hand since he was a boy down in Devon. But he couldn't argue with the thrill he got from holding Kate's hand. "I doubt it."

He didn't altogether understand the searching look that she directed at him. But then, he didn't understand so much about this encounter. Shelburn only understood that he was desperate to know this woman in every way he could. With a hankering that staggered him.

She took a sip of wine, as if she needed an extra dose of courage. "We've met before, you know."

"I don't believe it." Shock had him gaping at her. "I'd remember."

Her smile held a hint of teasing. "It was a long time ago."

Even deep in his cups, he would have noticed this remarkable woman. "I don't care."

"Do you recollect attending a house party at Rushby Hall in Lincolnshire, just before Christmas about fourteen years ago?"

He frowned. Plague take him, he didn't recall that. "I would have only been eighteen. And you must have been a child."

The smile continued to hover around those lush lips. Lips that he hadn't yet managed to taste. "Not quite. I was sixteen."

"And we danced?"

She shook her head. "I was well beneath your notice. I wasn't a comely adolescent."

He frowned. "That can't be so."

"That's very gallant, Leighton." Her fingers squeezed his. "But I'm afraid I was spotty and plump and tongue-tied. Or at least I was tongue-tied in that company. The other girls made me feel like a clodhopping interloper, unfit for anything higher than the servants' quarters."

"I like it when you say my name." He'd like it even better when she screamed it out in ecstasy. But right now, these unexpected revelations had him so intrigued that he almost didn't mind that he hadn't yet got her into bed.

Almost.

His frown deepened, as a distant memory stirred somewhere in the back of his mind. "We were there for the hunting."

"Yes."

"That would have been before I inherited the title. The pater didn't pass away until I was twenty-four."

"Yes, you were Viscount Lemaire."

The distant memory gained substance. "I was down from university for the Christmas holidays. James Rushby invited me and a crowd of his other friends to the family estate for some sport." Impetuous, good-hearted James Rushby, who had joined the Dragoon Guards and died at Vitoria three years ago. "Mary had a crowd of her chums there, too. But she was older than sixteen."

"She was friends with my sister Sylvie. They went to the same school."

"And you accompanied Sylvie." He had a dim recollection of two girls who always seemed on the edge of things. "Those friends of Mary's were little cats. I can't imagine they were kind to anyone they didn't count as sufficiently blue-blooded to enjoy their company."

"They weren't," Kate said, and he watched her hide a shudder, even so many years later. "But you were."

That didn't sound like him. He was a selfish bugger now, but he'd been worse when he was a stripling of eighteen. "It doesn't seem likely. When I was a lad, I thought the world had been created for my convenience."

She didn't smile. "You were the one everyone talked about. You were the one everyone wanted to be with. You should have heard how the girls gossiped about you. Even then, you were exciting and dangerous."

"I'm glad you thought so." By Jericho, he hoped that she continued to think that. At eighteen, he'd just been feeling his oats. He'd seduced one of Lord Rushby's neighbors, he now recalled. Susan? Susannah – that was her name. She'd been a kind and enthusiastic lover. It was a sign of his incurable shallowness that he'd forgotten her almost as soon as he left Lincolnshire. "So is that why you came with me today? To show all those nasty witches that you could get the man they wanted?"

He'd been well aware that those beady-eyed harpies were interested in him, but he'd kept his hands off. Even so young, he'd known to steer clear of Mary and her friends. Any dallying with a well-bred miss would see him caught in the parson's mousetrap before he had a chance to say, "Will you fuck me?"

In truth, he was a tad disappointed with Kate's reasons for taking up his invitation. Growing up alongside four sisters, he was awake to the games that girls played to get one up on their rivals. He hadn't imagined Kate was so petty. And however mean Mary's friends had been, it was a deuced long time to hold a grudge.

"Not at all." She waved her free hand in airy dismissal. "I didn't like those girls enough for them to leave any lasting wounds. I despised them as malicious nincompoops at least as much as they despised me for being a lowbred bumpkin."

Shelburn remained in the dark. "I'm sorry that I don't remember you."

He was. Although he suspected that back then, he wouldn't have had the experience to value Kate Starr for the jewel that she was.

"I didn't expect you would. But I remembered you."

"Because people talked about me?"

"No, of course not. What interest did I have in silly society games?"

"Kate, you'll have to be plain." He spread his hands in bewilderment. "I don't know what you're talking about."

"I didn't care for society games, but Sylvie did." Her eyes remained sad. "And those girls hurt her feelings, although heaven knows, after going to that awful school, she should have been used to snobbery. I've always been grateful that my parents decided to educate me at home. You might remember Sylvie. She was beautiful, like an angel. She had pale golden hair, and big blue eyes, and a smile that could light up a room. Not that she had much cause to smile at Rushby Hall. But you made her smile."

At last, at last, he recalled the details of that long ago house party, so exactly the same as every other house party that he'd attended over the years. "I danced with her. A waltz."

Approval lit Kate's eyes. "Yes, and that put all the cats' noses out of joint. You made Sylvie happy. Because you made Sylvie happy, you made me happy."

It was clear that Kate loved her sister, but when she said Sylvie was beautiful, it was no exaggeration. The girl had been exquisite, glowing like a lit candle. "Sylvie was lovely. The prettiest girl there by far."

Kate's approval deepened, which he liked, although elements of this tale troubled him in ways that he had difficulty defining. "Yes, she was. And sweet. She wasn't angry at the other girls like I was. She was just upset that they excluded us because we weren't nobly born."

He smiled. "I'm glad I made her happy, even if just for a moment." He hadn't been aware of the stakes when he'd asked Sylvie to waltz with him. He suspected that he just noticed a pretty girl and decided he'd like to hold her in his arms. "I assume she married long ago. I hope she's contented."

Kate's smile faltered, and to Shelburn's horror, tears glittered in her eyes. "She died a year later."

He felt sick. "Oh, hell, I'm sorry, Kate."

She pulled her hand free and brushed at her eyes. "She'd never been well, although she endured her difficulties with such courage and spirit. She was worth a thousand of those horrid women at Rushby Hall, who were so quick to belittle her. But I never saw her as happy as she was the night she danced with Viscount Lemaire. Afterward, she often spoke of that evening. You gave her a memory she cherished – and one I cherished, too. I never forgot your kindness."

All his misgivings coalesced into a foreboding that massed in his belly like jagged ice. He pushed away from the table and prowled across to the window to stare moodily outside. Anything to save him from seeing the radiance in Kate's gaze, as she talked about an act so insignificant to him that he'd forgotten about it until now.

"I'm glad I made her happy. It was little enough." It was. But it had been sufficient for Kate to make some highly inaccurate assessments about his character.

Right now, she wasn't sphinx-like at all. The admiration glowing in her eyes made him feel sick to the stomach.

Because while he was many things, he was no bloody hero.

She remained at the table but even with his back to her, he felt her gaze. "What's wrong, Shelburn?"

It shouldn't matter that she called him Shelburn instead of Leighton, but it did. He placed one hand on the window frame, as he battled the urge to punch a hole in the glass.

"You've cherished this memory for half your life. You've thought about it at night in your bed. You've compared my supposed gallantry to the actions of every man you've encountered." As his hand fisted against the paneled wood, bitterness edged his voice. "Then lo and behold, fate tosses you in my path when you least expect it. At last, all those dreams verge on becoming reality."

"Yes." Wariness edged her tone.

He turned to face her. "And you've convinced yourself you're in love with that chivalrous young man who rescued your beloved sister from social disaster. A young man you met once. A young man you didn't even speak to. And who you haven't seen in nigh on fourteen years."

She flushed with humiliation. If he truly was the kind, good fellow that she imagined him to be, he'd back down. "It was a harmless fantasy."

Nausea seethed in his gut as he shook his head. "No, it was calamitous. It's why you've never married. It why you're alone at thirty, when you could have a husband and children."

"Why are you being like this?" Her eyes flashed, as she surged to her feet. "What is it to you what happens in my head?"

"Because you're asking for trouble. Because I like you, Kate, and I fear I might hurt you." He struggled to get a grip on his temper. A temper unusual enough to make him pause. In general, he didn't care enough to get angry. "Because you think

I'm a knight in shining armor, when I wasn't that man then, and fourteen years of riotous self-indulgence mean I'm even less like that man now. You're falling victim to an illusion, and I refuse to take the blame when your ridiculous fancies come crashing up against nasty reality."

Her color receded as fast as it had risen, leaving her pale and stricken. "I haven't asked anything of you."

"No, you haven't. But does that mean you're not hoping for some fairy-tale ending to this escapade?" His eyes narrowed, and his tone turned frigid. "I'm no Prince Charming, Miss Starr. I'm a ruthless, heartless seducer whose only purpose in life is the satisfaction of his own appetites. Under the circumstances, I believe it's time I took you back to London."

CHAPTER SEVEN

Kate stared aghast at the stony-faced stranger standing in front of her, while anger – and dismay – roiled inside her. Most of the anger was directed at herself. What on earth had she been thinking?

Damn her loose tongue. Damn the fact that Leighton was smart enough to read between the lines of what she'd said.

She was such a fool. So far, the attraction building between them had been playful. But she'd dared to venture beyond that game, and her chances of becoming Lord Shelburn's lover crumbled to ash.

Only now that this opportunity threatened to disappear did she admit how relieved she was to escape what awaited in London.

When she replied, her voice was as cold as his. "You're wrong about me."

Not, to her chagrin, wrong about everything, but about enough for her to claw back a little pride. She loathed the way that he'd mocked her romantic fantasies, however absurd they might be.

One eyebrow lifted in sardonic enquiry. "Am I?"

She squared her shoulders and raised her chin. "As you pointed out, our one encounter took place many years ago, when I was a silly schoolgirl. I'm no longer a silly schoolgirl. I'm a grown woman with experience of the world and business. I'm not expecting a fairy tale. I'm not expecting anything of you, except pleasure and passion, and I hope a little respect and consideration. A wedding ring isn't part of our bargain."

He didn't look reassured, blast him. "If you're not harboring notions of love, why did you come with me?"

How she wished he'd stop saying "love" in that vilely snide way, as if the mere concept was an utter impossibility.

Kate hesitated to confide in him again, after the disastrous consequences last time, so she kept her answer simple. "I'm not looking for love. I'm looking for adventure."

"An adventure that will change your life forever." He didn't sound impressed with her declaration. "If I enter into yet another affair, the world will shrug its shoulders. But should our association be discovered, you'll lose your reputation. I imagine running the mills as a single woman has been hard. It will be impossible when everyone you're dealing with is sniggering about you spreading your legs for an unregenerate rake."

His frankness made her flinch. Although she acknowledged that he was right.

Which didn't mean that she intended to forego this chance. The irony was that he claimed to be selfish to the bone, yet he obviously cared about what happened to her once they parted.

Kate sighed and gestured to the armchairs in front of the fire. "Please stop glowering at me. It's making me nervous."

He didn't accept her invitation to sit down. "*You're* making me nervous."

"Why? What is it to you if I emerge from this affair chastened if wiser?" she responded with some heat. "You must have broken hearts before."

"Not as many as you'd think. The women I pursue are sophisticated creatures. In general, hearts aren't at issue."

"I'm not so green as—"

"Yes, you are. At least when it comes to sharing a man's bed." Leighton went on with a certainty that made her cringe. "You mentioned respect and consideration. I'd lack both if I led you to believe that our liaison will be anything but two adults coming together for a brief time because they desire each other. There is no future for us."

"You're very blunt." She couldn't help feeling hurt, even though he told her nothing that she didn't already know.

Despite his shrug, she knew that his feelings were far from casual. "It's for your own good."

A bleak smile quirked her lips. "Whenever someone says that to me, I know I'm in for a disagreeable experience."

He didn't smile back. "Kate, doesn't this seem mad to you? You don't know me. I could be a violent brute. I could be a drunkard. I could be a murderer. Good God, I could be a complete bore. Yet you're willing to take such chances."

Once more, warmth rose to her cheeks, although she usually wasn't a blusher. She'd learned young to hide any feminine vulnerabilities. They only put her at a disadvantage, when she dealt with colleagues and business rivals.

At least Leighton wasn't calling her Miss Starr in that horrid, haughty tone anymore. That had cut like a razor. He sounded more like the charming companion who had driven her from London, thank goodness.

Now that he brought her girlish fantasies into the light, they did sound preposterous. But something obstinate inside Kate wouldn't give up the conviction that he was a better man than he admitted.

Which didn't mean that she expected the Earl of Shelburn to fall in love with her. There was no chance of that, she knew.

"I don't want to go back to London." Her voice was flat. "I want to stay here and find out what you've learned from all those shameless ladies you've seduced over the years."

"Even if that stops you finding a decent man to marry?"

Her shoulders slumped as grim reality thumped down on top of her. "I've found a decent man to marry."

Surprise flared in his eyes. "Have you indeed?"

Her gesture was dismissive. "The problem is—"

"You don't want to marry him."

"No."

"So when the man you'd dreamed of for so long, however little those dreams had to do with real life—"

"Please don't belabor the point."

"I won't. You must realize by now that I'm not at all the kind of fellow a girl should idealize."

Actually he remained that fellow, however many unwelcome shocks this conversation might contain. She'd become wise enough, however, to keep that observation to herself.

He went on. "At the Angel, you thought that heaven had offered you a reprieve."

"Yes."

This time, he waved toward the chairs. "Won't you tell me?"

"Why should you care?" It was her turn to ignore the invitation. "You don't need to know the details of my life. On your own admission, this affair will be brief. If it ever happens at all."

For the first time in what felt like an eon, his smile was genuine. "I have a feeling it's going to happen."

"But first, you want to make sure there are no more nasty revelations." Kate didn't know why she was needling him. After all, she didn't want him taking her back to London.

"Perhaps." He didn't contradict her insulting description of her penchant for him. Yet again, she wished that she'd thought before revealing so much. "But won't you sit down? I'll feel less like we're adversaries."

She didn't shift. "What are we instead?"

"I'm waiting to find out."

That sounded promising. Perhaps she hadn't spoiled all her chances of sharing his bed. It would be a damnable shame if, having decided to sacrifice her chastity, she left this inn as pure as she'd arrived.

"Very well," she said and crossed to sink into a chair. She'd told him so much already –and he'd guessed a lot of what she hadn't said – that she might as well tell him the rest.

Leighton hadn't apologized for upsetting her. Why would he, when he believed that he was in the right? But as she watched him pour the last of the claret into their glasses and carry them across, she was relieved that he'd conquered his temper.

"Thank you," she said quietly, accepting the wine.

He sat in the other chair and studied her with a brooding attention that made her shift against the cushioned seat. Without diverting his gaze, he raised his glass for a sip. "Tell me."

She sighed again and set her untouched wine on the occasional table between the two chairs. "His name is Jebediah Williams. He's a manufacturer and mine owner from Manchester. His businesses and mine dovetail in a way that will work to our mutual benefit. My cousin Alfred, the man you saw at the Angel, favors the match."

"Does your cousin have power over you?"

She shook her head. "No. I took my cousins into my home after my father's death, in part to help with the mill and in part to provide me with a respectable living situation. Young women don't live alone, if they wish to preserve their good name, especially when they deal with men all day every day."

As she'd expected, Leighton didn't miss the sour note. "It's the way of the world."

"That doesn't make it any easier to bear, when Hazel is a scatterbrain and Alfred can be a pompous bully." Never more so than when it came to this marriage. "Alfred met Mr. Williams at a scientific lecture and came back all fired up to arrange a merger."

"But why does a merger mean becoming the rogue's wife?"

"Mr. Williams isn't a rogue. He's a respectable and successful businessman. And the idea of a wedding came later." She bit back a sigh. "I only agreed to consider his proposal when he said that he was willing to sign an agreement to leave me in charge of Starr Mills. The settlement papers confirm me as sole manager, unless illness leaves me incapable of fulfilling my duties."

"How romantic."

Her lips tightened. "You don't believe in romance."

"No, but you do." When she didn't respond to that – she'd suffered quite enough mockery today, thank you – he went on. "I'm assuming he's older than you."

"Yes, he's close to fifty. He lost his first wife twenty years ago, and he has a grown family. He's a good, sensible, clever man, with some excellent ideas for expanding our enterprises."

If she heard the lack of enthusiasm in her voice, Leighton would, too. "No doubt. The answer to a maiden's prayer."

The irony in his tone made her prickle. "I am a maiden – and you know exactly who I was praying for and how unsuitable he is. Mr. Williams is steady and practical, and he won't expect love."

She was grateful that he didn't remark on her admission that she dreamed of him. "So why are you here with my unworthy self instead of hanging on this paragon's every word?"

Kate couldn't help feeling that it was unfair for Leighton to disdain her for being too romantic, then criticize her pragmatism. She couldn't win. "Because I'd backed myself into a corner I didn't want to be in."

The earl studied her as if she belonged to a strange new species. "I refuse to believe that an attractive woman can't do better than a middle-aged widower, however adept in business."

"Thank you," she said, although the mortifying truth was that she only felt attractive when Leighton devoured her with his eyes.

"You're beautiful and you're plump in the pocket. There must have been offers from younger, more eligible men. A man your own age who gives you a chance at emotional fulfillment, aside from worldly advantages."

He was right. Over the years, she hadn't lacked for offers. When she inherited the mills, an army of suitors had besieged her. Whether her swains were interested in her or the factories, she couldn't say. It didn't matter. She had no intention of marrying any of them. Her determined and long-standing refusal of all proposals meant that over recent years, the pursuit had faded away.

"Perhaps, but none of my younger suitors were willing to leave me a free hand with the mills. Most men believe a woman's place is in the home, not exposing herself to the hurly-burly of the commercial world."

"Ah."

Her bitterness sharpened. "They call me the ice queen and unnatural and the Amazon of Bradbourne. Although none of the cruel names stopped those men from doing business with me, much as they might prefer to deal with a male. Even if Alfred was present at negotiations, I made it clear I was in charge."

"Alfred mustn't have liked that."

"He didn't. But he's well paid, and he feels a family obligation to me. Apart from Alfred and his wife Hazel, I'm alone in the world."

"If you marry Williams, that will change."

She hid a shudder. In her one brief meeting with Mr. Williams's children, they'd made it obvious that they didn't approve of his matrimonial plans.

"Yes." She sipped her wine. It was a surprising relief to talk about all this with a neutral party. For months, she'd chased decisions around her head. Ever since Mr. Williams had visited Bradbourne to tour her largest mill and ended the day by proposing.

"So you came to London to marry him?"

"Yes. We were to move into his house tonight, then sign the settlement documents tomorrow. The wedding was to take place on Friday."

"It's not too late to bring your plans to fruition." Leighton, like her, must have registered her use of the past tense. "It sounds like Williams chose you for mercenary reasons, not love. If you go back and say you surrendered to an impulse that you've since regretted, I'm sure he'll forgive you."

Kate muffled another sigh. She suspected that Leighton was right. "But I no longer believe I can stomach such a bloodless bargain. When you beckoned to me across that innyard, I recognized that I'd let Alfred nag me into this marriage. I'd given up on life, but there was more out there than settling for a loveless union with a man I respected but could never love."

"So that's why you came with me," Shelburn said in dawning realization.

"You were right about it seeming like a message from fate."

"But a message telling you to break out for freedom, not because of some mawkish notion of a lad you met half a lifetime ago."

Kate wasn't going to admit to it anyway. "It told me to keep hold of my dreams, despite well-meaning people convinced they had a better idea for what I should do."

"What will you do, now you've decided against having Williams?"

She set her wine down on the table. "My old governess lives outside Stevenage in a village called Heddle End. After I leave the Merry Haymaker, I'll go and stay with Miss Donald for a couple of days. That will give me a chance to consider my next step."

Whatever else she did, her return to Bradbourne would mean smoothing a lot of ruffled feathers. Hazel would be in a flap, and Alfred would be offended that she'd broken an engagement he was so eager to promote.

Most of all, she needed to apologize to Mr. Williams. She'd behaved badly toward him. Unforgivably, in fact.

"You don't look happy."

"I'm just thinking of the mess waiting for me when I go back to my real life." Kate stiffened her shoulders, as if she already faced the hullabaloo. "I'll manage."

She'd managed when Sylvie died. And Mother. And Da. She'd clawed a place for herself at the mills, against oceans of masculine disapproval.

Before she'd inherited, her father's ill health had started to affect profitability. But since then, she'd built the enterprise into a thriving concern. Clearing up the chaotic aftermath of her failed engagement paled in comparison with what she'd already achieved.

"Of course you will."

"That declaration rings a little false." His confidence made her frown. "Not long ago, you called me a complete henwit."

He grimaced. "I was rather rough."

She supposed that was as close to an apology as he was likely to come. "You were."

"I was appalled that the rocks of idiotic sentiment were about to scupper a promising affair."

Idiotic sentiment? Did Kate need any greater proof that Leighton despised love, in spite of his efforts to unite Lady Verena and Lord Colville?

Or perhaps Leighton only despised love when it applied to him.

"As you made more than clear," she said flatly.

He had the grace to look embarrassed. "You mightn't believe it, but I'm famous for my tact."

"You're right. I don't believe it."

Except that she did. As a young man, he'd been the epitome of charm and social polish. The mature man might display a few harder edges, but he was charming, too. At least until Kate scared all the savoir faire out of him with mention of that forbidden topic, love.

"I can't blame you. Do you want to leave? I'm happy to drive you to your governess. Stevenage is only a couple of hours away. Before the day is out, I can have you tucked up in a chaste bed with your virtue intact. Just because I offered you a means of escape, you don't owe me anything."

No, no, no. "Do you want me to go?"

The offer of a quick trip back to London retained its sting. But nowhere near as much as it stung to think that these few hours were all she'd have of him.

He was wrong to say that she'd hoped he'd fall in love with her. She wasn't such a noodle. One of the kingdom's most eligible bachelors was never going to make a lifelong commitment to a middle-class woman of no distinction and well past first youth. That sort of thing didn't even happen in fairy tales.

"I was in a bit of a state when I said that." Self-deprecation firmed his lips. "When I said I'm happy to take you back to London, I was exaggerating. In fact, I was a damned liar. I'd like you to stay, that is if you understand my terms. But the decision of whether you become my lover, my dear Miss Starr, remains yours."

CHAPTER EIGHT

Nobody had ever looked at Shelburn the way that Kate Starr did. As if she could see right through the surface polish to the real man beneath.

He hoped to Hades that she did see a real man there. He'd spent so many years living on the most superficial of levels, he wouldn't wager a groat that she did.

Most of the people he knew were more than happy to deal with his debonair outer shell. Verena was his closest friend, and even she never attempted to plumb his soul. Perhaps because her own soul concealed secrets that she'd rather hide from the light of day.

Kate might look deep, yet she harbored the illusion that he was a better man than he was. He'd flinched away from the sickly hero worship that he'd heard in her voice when she spoke about him dancing with her sister. When he'd seen something that might be love in her eyes, he'd been horrified. Men like him didn't play with such dangerous emotions.

Shelburn should consign her to Jericho. He would, if he didn't want her so much. While Leighton Anstey might be no knight in shining armor, he had the brains to obey that imperious hunger.

As she considered her answer, she went back to being a sphinx. That lovely face gave nothing away.

Only a madwoman would cling to such a ludicrous penchant. Kate struck him as one of the sanest people that he'd ever met. Now he thought about it, he made sense of what she'd said. Even better, he could live with the conclusions that he reached.

Shelburn suspected that she'd used his face for her forbidden fantasies. By day, she had to be all business, suppressing any sensual impulses. But by night, she could release every wanton imagining. His masculine instincts, honed during years of bed sport, told him that a current of passion ran strong beneath her composure.

What luck that they'd met at the Angel. For both of them.

It had saved her from a disastrous union. It gave him the chance to feed appetites that beggared previous experience. Even this suspense now, as he waited for her to offer him the keys to heaven, was new.

When she gave a short nod, as though she'd resolved an internal argument, his heart crashed against his ribs in overpowering relief. "I'd prefer to stay. After this, I doubt that I'll ever marry, so it would be nice to discover what it's like to share a man's bed."

While Shelburn should be overjoyed, he couldn't suppress a twinge of pique. "I'd like you to stay because you want me, not just because you're curious about intercourse."

Her lips twitched. "I didn't want to risk you flying up into the boughs again."

He frowned. "I don't want love. But desire? Desire makes life worth living."

It was true, although over recent years, he'd gone through the motions rather than responded to genuine need. When he looked at Kate, he felt genuine need. Need that thundered in his blood like a stormy ocean.

"Then I'm eager to discover it with you."

Satisfaction settled in his gut as he rose and crossed to ring for the servants. "Then let's ensure our privacy for the rest of the day. And night."

Within a quarter of an hour, the remains of their meal had been cleared away. Decanters of claret and brandy were arrayed on the sideboard, along with dishes of nuts and crackers and sweetmeats. As the hours passed, he and Kate would need to fuel their passion.

After the last servant closed the door behind him, Shelburn heaved a sigh of heartfelt relief. Every minute that they'd bustled around had felt like an hour.

He burned to take Kate into his arms and show her everything that she'd missed. "Alone at last," he said with theatrical emphasis that in no way understated his desperation.

Kate glanced up from where she sat on the window seat. The afternoon sun poured through and revealed a woman so damned beautiful that she took his breath away.

It staggered Shelburn that this glorious creature was as untouched as any of the chits who flocked to London each season in search of a husband. What the devil was wrong with the men of Bradbourne? Did they all have water in their veins instead of good red blood?

"Should we go into the bedroom?" For once, her impressive control showed signs of cracking.

"Not straightaway."

Tenderness filled him, as he recognized that even if she'd fantasized about him for fourteen long years, inexperience had restricted her flights of fancy. At least when she surrendered to her imaginings after they parted, she'd have more to work with.

He shoved aside the thought of her going away. They hadn't spoken about how long they intended to stay together, but neither anticipated a lengthy liaison. For pity's sake, Kate wouldn't even venture beyond Hertfordshire in his company. She planned to go and stay with a governess who lived nearby. That alone argued that she meant to remain with him for a couple of days at most.

Nor had he prepared for a long absence when he left London. Neither of them even had a change of linen with them.

Nonetheless the idea of Kate's departure made his gut tighten in rejection.

She surveyed the room in puzzlement. "You want to...do it here?"

"We could."

Her eyes rounded with an astonishment that made him laugh. "We could?"

The room was full of places where he could seduce her. That window seat, for example. And he knew from previous visits that the armchairs were sturdy enough for a vigorous fuck. Not to mention a floor and four walls, and a low-backed settle that he could bend her over while he took her from behind.

But he sensed that if he suggested anything too outré, she'd only become more skittish. "Later. Bed offers us plenty of scope for our first encounter."

She subjected him to another of those searching inspections. "My goodness, you really are wicked. I had no idea."

Shelburn laughed again and stepped forward to stand in front of her. "Let's start with the basics."

"Won't you be bored with the basics?" Her hands twined in her lap. "I fear I've joined a game where I'm not up to the standard of play."

"I'll help you learn the ropes." He smiled down at her in delight. "I'm sure you'll find your way."

She didn't look reassured. "I hope so."

"Come, Kate. The woman brave enough to step into my carriage is brave enough to explore the attraction between us." His smile widened. "I don't require a hundred exotic variations. I want you so much that all I need is you."

That didn't seem to provide much reassurance. He saw her mind working at top speed to piece together what they might do to each other. "A hundred?"

"We'll start with one and see where we go from there." Although already his head whirled with images of Kate on her knees and taking his cock into her mouth. Or riding him like a jockey set on winning the Derby.

Heat flushed his body, and anticipation tightened his balls. God help him, at this rate, it would be a miracle if he lasted long enough to get her into the bed. Anything esoteric asked too much of his frail control.

The pity of it was that he had to be careful with her. Kate was an innocent, unused to a man's touch. She was brave and spirited, but this conversation made it clear – as if it wasn't clear already – that she was a novice when it came to passion.

"If you say so," she said faintly. Color lined her cheekbones as she focused on the front of his breeches.

"I told you I wanted you."

"So I see." She tried and failed to match his dry tone. "Should I...should I take off my clothes?"

The craving to rip away that modest blue gown hurtled through him. "In time."

She made a baffled gesture. "What should I do instead?"

Holding out his hand, he kept his voice gentle. "I thought we might begin with a kiss."

"A kiss?" she said, as if the word made no sense.

Incredulity slammed him. Was she even more untouched than he'd thought? "Kate, haven't you ever been kissed?"

"I have."

"And?"

She wrinkled her nose in a way that charmed him. "I didn't much like it. It was wet and nasty, and the boy's breath smelled of onions."

He burst out laughing. "Good God, that sounds ghastly."

She gave an eloquent shudder. "It was."

"I'll try to wipe away the unpleasant memory."

"The fault may have been mine. Edward Carruthers was counted as quite the local lothario."

"More and more, I despair of the men of Derbyshire. I'm glad that you waited for me. They're unworthy of you."

Her eyebrows arched, as she accepted his hand and rose to her feet with a grace that made his heart swoop. "And you are worthy of me?"

She was close enough for him to catch her scent. Cedar instead of flowers, because of the soap that the inn supplied. Beneath that, something warm and enticing that was familiar after sitting beside her in his phaeton.

"At least I know how to kiss a woman."

"Edward Carruthers thought he did, too."

Retaining her hand, Shelburn cupped that determined jaw with his other hand. She wasn't a delicate woman, a sweet little doll. Something in him loved her strength. She might bend, but she'd never break.

Kate started at the contact, and her gaze flew up to meet his. He read uncertainty there, an uncertainty that she did her best to hide with humor. He imagined that she was used to pretending calmness and self-reliance. That façade had allowed a young girl to take charge of the mills after her father's death.

More strength. Back then, sharks must have been circling to rip her to shreds and steal her inheritance.

Under his fingers, her skin was soft and smooth. Shelburn traced a line down her cheek and tilted her face up. He was right to think that she was nervous. She trembled under his touch.

"Kate?" he murmured.

"Yes?"

He smiled with a tenderness that he didn't have to feign. "Give me your mouth."

Before she could answer, he lowered his head. As his lips sank into cushiony softness, he caught a sweet gust of breath. Yet again, she jumped, although she must have expected him to kiss her sooner or later. After all, he'd announced his intentions what felt like a century ago.

The soft moan that escaped her didn't sound like a denial. It sounded like curiosity. After a moment, her lips moved in response to the light pressure of his.

He nipped her lower lip and sucked it into his mouth for an instant. She tasted of salty honey. A flavor that he feared might become addictive.

This time, her incoherent little mutter expressed surprise.

Shelburn lifted his head, knowing that if he continued, he'd forget that he meant to proceed slowly, coaxing her through each step so he didn't frighten her. By God, that was the most innocent kiss that he'd shared since he'd hit puberty. Odd that it turned his knees to water in a way that his most carnal recent encounters had failed to do.

Kate had closed her eyes. Now she raised heavy eyelids and surveyed his face. For a long moment, he drowned in glorious green and gold. For once, she looked dazed and not at all self-possessed.

He didn't mistake what she gave him today. Not just her virginity, but a trust that he swore he wouldn't betray. Despite the masculine urge to seize and possess.

He'd promised himself when they drove up from London that he'd rattle her poise. He should have realized even then that if he did, maintaining his own detachment would prove impossible.

Because the temptation to ask for more was so strong, he released her face and stepped back. It was either that or sweep her into his arms and through to the bedroom. She wasn't ready for that.

"That was..." she whispered.

He smiled. "Better than Edward Carruthers?"

She blinked the mist away from her eyes. "No onions at all."

"I'm glad. Would you like to do it again?"

"Yes, please."

Reminding himself to be careful, Shelburn framed her waist with shaking hands. This time, she raised her chin in unmistakable invitation.

She didn't need to ask twice. His grip firmed, and this time, his lips lingered. She responded with a seeking pressure of her own. As she softened in his grasp, she released a husky little sigh of surrender. He dared to flick his tongue against her lips.

She stiffened and pulled away, gasping. "Leighton?"

He smiled, enchanted anew, although until today, he wouldn't have said that innocence had any particular appeal. But something about showing Kate the joy that she could find with a man touched his rusty heart.

There was such a provocative contrast between the smart, capable woman she was out in the world and the curious, untried, vulnerable creature she became in his arms.

"Open your mouth for me. I want to taste you."

She looked startled. "That sounds bizarre."

"Nonetheless I think you'll like it."

"Is there…is there anything else I should be doing?"

"Well, you could put your arms around me. I'd like that very much."

His hands flexed around her supple waist, as he couldn't help thinking about some other things that he'd like her to do.

"Very well." She sounded uncertain.

She rested her hands on his shoulders. Her touch overturned his heart in a most disconcerting fashion, and he released a ragged exhalation.

Kate wasn't paying attention to his reactions. Instead, with excruciating slowness, she slid her palms down the front of his coat before spreading them wide. For a charged moment, one hand rested over the place where his heart pounded with excitement.

"You feel so powerful," she murmured as if she spoke to herself. "It makes me quite swoony."

Shelburn's head was spinning, too. And so far, all she'd done was touch him through three layers of clothing. Heaven help him when they were naked together.

"You're so tall." She spoke in that same soft, musing tone. "I'm used to towering over most of the men I know. I never thought any man could make me feel all clingy and feminine. But you do."

He swallowed to clear a throat jammed with excitement and a poignant emotion that he couldn't put a name to. With every second, his determination to play by his usual rules became more threadbare. "By all means, cling."

She gave a faint huff of laughter as her hands retraced their path up to his shoulders, then ventured higher until they linked behind his neck. "You'd hate that. You know you would."

In most cases, he'd agree with her. But the idea of Kate Starr turning to him satisfied some primitive male urge. Right now, with her so close, he liked the idea of her finding shelter in his strength and treating him like a hero. Which was odd, given his reaction to the news that she was in love with him. Or a false version of him at any rate.

Stop it. You're nobody's hero. You're the worst lord in London.

But the reprimand lost all force, when he stared into Kate's unforgettable face. Shelburn feared that for the first time in his life, he was in danger of making a fool of himself over a woman.

He didn't know what she saw in his expression, but he heard her breath catch and she swayed closer. Excitement surged, and he lashed his arms around her.

He took her mouth with an urgency that made no allowance for inexperience. With a muffled moan, she curved to fit his body. Elation flooded him, as he realized that she...*clung*.

This time, when his tongue traced her closed lips, she opened to him.

CHAPTER NINE

The pleasure eclipsed any disagreeable memories of Edward Carruthers. Leighton's lips on hers were all skilled seduction as they slanted across Kate's.

When he silently requested access, she parted in helpless surrender. Even though it seemed a peculiar thing for him to want to do.

The sudden intimacy shocked her, made her recoil for an instant, before his tongue slid against hers in what she could only describe as a caress. Every qualm dissolved under waves of sensual heat.

When she moved her tongue in answer, he rewarded her with a growl of approval and brought her closer. The height and power that she found so intoxicating were even more overwhelming, now she was in his arms. Despite his urgent kisses, he held her with a tenderness that made her feel safe and fragile and...*cherished*.

The kiss became a playful dance, even as the rush of response turned into a throbbing need that settled between her legs. The sensation was disturbing and pleasurable at the same time.

Was this desire? She was too inexperienced to be sure. But she was sure that she'd die if Leighton stopped kissing her.

As the pressure of his lips deepened, he pulled her closer until she felt every hard line of his body. He growled and buried one hand in her hair, bringing her face nearer and changing the angle of the kiss.

This thrilling variation had her knees threatening to collapse. To keep her balance, Kate hooked her hands over his broad shoulders. It was a delicious relief to lean, if just for a moment, into someone else's strength.

All the time, Leighton's mouth tantalized and tormented her. Thrill after thrill rocked her, as that powerful yearning in the pit of her stomach built to an unbearable intensity.

When he raised his head and stared down at her with glittering dark eyes, she felt as if he'd made her anew. With a kiss! By the time she tumbled into bed with him, she wouldn't recognize herself.

"That was..." she began, stepping back on wobbly legs and raising an unsteady hand to lips that felt swollen and tingling.

Marvelous? Astonishing? Magnificent? Life-changing?

But she recalled how he'd reacted to her ill-timed confidences earlier, so she chose a less contentious adjective. "...unexpected."

His laugh held a note of fondness, that she knew she couldn't pay too much heed to. One eyebrow quirked. "But nice?"

"Definitely nice." She wanted to hold onto him. Heaven help her, she wanted him to kiss her again. Instead, she flattened her hand on the wall behind her.

"Nice enough to venture a little further?"

"Yes." It was almost unbearable to contemplate the sad fact that she'd waited until she was thirty to experience a real kiss. Although at least there was some compensation in knowing that when it happened, she was in a master's hands.

What else might that master show her? Anticipation spiked. She'd find out before too much longer.

His smile turned down at the corners. "If you keep looking at me like that, I won't be responsible for my actions."

She slumped against the wall, continuing to devour him with her eyes. "I can't help it," she admitted breathlessly.

By heaven, he was so handsome. He retained the pure bone structure that she remembered from that beautiful boy she'd met so long ago. But the mature man was a thousand times more compelling. Her gaze drank in the tousled dark hair and the way one lock tumbled over his high forehead. His mouth was fuller than usual, and the intensity of his expression made her stomach clench with excitement.

Her giddy heart, already racing as if it wanted to escape the confines of her chest, somersaulted as she watched him raise his hands to the elaborate neckcloth.

"Damn it," he muttered, as he fumbled untying the knot.

A smug smile curved Kate's lips. How gratifying to think that extraordinary kiss left him addle-headed as well. She straightened and stepped forward. "Let me help."

His hands fell away to hang loose at his sides. She sucked in a deep breath as she moved within reach. To her surprise, her touch was deft. Kate loosened the neckcloth and let it drift to the red and yellow rug on the floor.

She inhaled. Leighton smelled marvelous, like everything good in life. She imprinted that scent on her senses, determined never to forget it.

As she moved to unbutton his coat and the cream silk waistcoat beneath it, he gave a grunt of amusement. "The rake is overcome, and the innocent is as cool as a cucumber. You're a marvel, Kate Starr."

Again, she reminded herself not to give the tender tone too much significance. Although she couldn't mistake that right now, she received his wholehearted approval. She liked that. But even as she verged closer to becoming Leighton's lover, she had to remember that while he might want her now, there was no guarantee that he'd want her tomorrow.

She had to make today count and cast aside any thought for the future. Difficult for a woman who preferred to plan, but not impossible. Especially if all the rewards turned out to be as wonderful as his kisses.

"I've wasted so much time." Her hands slid up to push the elegant dark blue coat from his shoulders. It felt odd to have to stretch to do that. The wicked notion struck her that when they lay down together, their bodies would fit together perfectly.

Mr. Williams was tall, too. She crushed the thought as soon as it arose. Her issues with her betrothed held no place in this quiet, sunlit room. She was interested in one man right now, and it wasn't Jebediah Williams.

She turned and laid the coat over the back of an armchair. Even in her impatience, she couldn't forget that fine Savile Row tailoring deserved careful treatment. No mill owner's daughter, however distracted, would ever disrespect quality cloth.

Leighton closed his eyes and groaned. "You're killing me."

She smiled and dropped her gaze to his breeches. "You look fighting fit to me."

When he noticed the direction of her glance, he smiled with male appreciation. She'd already realized that he approved of her boldness.

She returned to remove his unbuttoned waistcoat and lay it on top of the coat. How marvelous he looked, with his loose white shirt open over his chest. She caught a glimpse of crisp black curls and a strong throat. He was such a virile man.

He hauled the shirt over his head and flung it to the ground. Kate's calmness took a jolt as she surveyed the muscled expanse of his chest and shoulders. Whorls of dark hair covered his firm pectorals and traced a line down the center of his torso to disappear beneath the waistband of his breeches.

His rod swelled against the front fall. She'd felt that insistent flesh against her when they kissed, but now all the moisture dried from her mouth.

She'd never seen a naked man. She very much wanted to see Leighton without a stitch of clothing. But trepidation mixed with curiosity. Even under his breeches, he looked very large.

He groaned again and stepped closer. "Are you all right?"

She licked parched lips and dragged her eyes upward. "I'm feeling swoony again."

He laughed, and he was still laughing as his lips captured hers once more. He nipped gently until she opened again. She curled her arms around him and drowned in dark heat, as within an instant, the kiss moved from teasing to voracious.

She felt his hands in her hair, then gasped into his mouth when she felt a heavy sliding weight. Her long hair tumbled down around her shoulders. Leighton drew away to run his fingers through the thick, waving mass. The wonder in his face made her wayward heart cramp.

"Beautiful," he sighed, lifting a hank. With a languorous relish that warmed her blood, he let the tress fall in a slow cascade. "I thought it would be."

Another painful constriction of her heart. She loved the pleasure he took in her. It made her feel less at a disadvantage. It fed a soul that had closed itself away for too long to everything but common sense and the demands of business.

Kate released a breath that she felt like she'd been holding since Sylvie died. Here she wasn't formidable Miss Starr. Here she was just Kate. Soon she'd become Leighton's Kate.

He rested his cheek on hers, her hair a silky veil between skin and skin. The desire rising between them had felt desperate and urgent. But all of a sudden, time slowed to spin out in long golden threads of delight. She sank into a radiant new world, redolent with the rich scent of a healthy male.

When his fingers plucked at the hooks down the back of her dress, she pressed nearer and closed her eyes. His hands seemed to have regained their dexterity. She felt a sudden looseness as he untied the belt cinching the dress under her breasts.

"Goodness me, that was impressive," she murmured, keeping her face hidden in his shoulder. "You did all that without looking."

She felt as much as heard the low rumble of his amusement. "There's an advantage to choosing a rake as a lover."

"More than one, I hope."

When he brushed her sleeves down her arms, she shivered in anticipation. "Step back and I'll take off your dress."

She didn't move to obey. "I've never taken my clothes off for a man before."

"Are you shy?"

"A little."

"You could help," he suggested, with that gentle irony that always charmed her.

"I think you're managing fine on your own."

Another of those subterranean laughs. "Very well."

With sudden purpose, he tugged her dress until it slithered over her hips and crumpled to the floor in a dark blue heap.

"Oh." Despite her mockery, she admired his efficiency.

He stepped back, eyes alight with an interest that made her skin tingle. "My dear Miss Starr, what an unexpected – and intriguing – surprise."

Her cheeks heated as she glanced down. Only her modiste in Sheffield and her maid knew her secret. And now Leighton. "It seems a harmless enough extravagance."

"The very respectable Miss Starr has a penchant for naughty undergarments." He sounded marvelously pleased with events.

"I'd say frivolous rather than naughty," she said in a faint voice.

With a deliberate movement, he shook his head. "I wouldn't."

His gaze burned as it ran over her half corset of burgundy silk, embroidered with twining gold vines and flowers. The way the corset pushed her breasts up seemed to rivet Leighton's attention.

That concentrated survey made her nipples tighten under the rose silk shift. She needed him to touch her there. She needed it more than her next breath.

Kate made a helpless gesture. "There's something about—"

"About being all business on the surface, while you're dressed like a courtesan beneath."

She could imagine that he was well acquainted with what a professional seductress wore beneath her dress. "I wouldn't quite say that," she said, shifting in discomfort.

The soft friction her drawers set up between her thighs only heightened her arousal. She felt hot and damp and needy down there in a most unsettling way.

It seemed mad to be so disturbed, when he wasn't even touching her. Except that blazing inspection felt like the brush of his hands on her skin.

"I love it," he said, and she realized that he'd noticed her embarrassment. How could he not? She must be the color of a ripe strawberry. "It's what I should have expected. You're a woman of endless temptations, but a man has to take the time and trouble to see the full picture."

"That doesn't sound too flattering."

His smile was so wolfish that a shudder jolted her, a powerful combination of apprehension and anticipation. "Oh, it's flattering, all right. You offer a lover a banquet of spectacular surprises. I'm the luckiest man in the world."

That could be meaningless flattery, except that she couldn't mistake his enthusiasm. He liked discovering that beneath her modest frock, she indulged less prosaic tastes. He liked it very much indeed.

That gave her the courage to raise her chin and stand proudly under his thorough inspection.

Despite knowing that the cobweb-thin shift revealed every line of her body.

Without shifting his attention from her, he backed to drop into a chair and take off his boots.

"Shall I unhook my stays?" she asked, surprised at how collected she sounded.

"Not yet." That hungry smile lingered on his lips. "Sit down and let me take off your shoes and stockings."

She subjected him to a questioning regard. "You don't seem to be in a hurry anymore."

When his eyes met hers, she read endless craving. "Such a fine banquet deserves savoring."

Kate didn't trust his words. He must have used pretty compliments to woo many a hesitant lover. "I hope when the time comes, you don't feel like you're eating plain bread and cheese."

He laughed. "I'm very partial to bread and cheese. But I have a feeling you're going to be everything spicy and delicious, a feast for the senses."

She had her doubts. After all, he must have tangled with women who knew every sensual art. But on the other hand, he wanted her, she wanted him. That would have to be enough. She wasn't about to step back from this chance.

Without further demurrals, she crossed to sit in the armchair before the fire.

Leighton kneeled in front of her. When Kate cradled his face, his cheeks were warm under her palms. Although he'd shaved before their meal, his whiskers prickled.

For a long moment, she searched his features, trying to read his soul. Although given that this was a fleeting encounter between two strangers, souls shouldn't matter.

But the feelings that she'd nurtured, however futile, made her seek more in this man than the careless rake. She wasn't fool enough to imagine that what they were about to do would change his life the way it would change hers. But she couldn't bear thinking that he lent her surrender no more significance than he'd give to a bet on the turn of a card or a quick dinner snatched on a journey.

He called her mysterious, but she found mystery upon mystery layered behind those dark eyes. This wasn't a man who ceded his secrets just for the asking. Somewhere deep in that gaze, she thought she caught an urgency that hinted this was important to him now, if not in the future.

So when she kissed him, she didn't restrain the tenderness that sweetened her ardor to something more poignant than mere appetite.

She met tenderness in his response. Perhaps a tenderness wrapped in desire, but present all the same. What surprised her was that he didn't take control, the way he had with their earlier kisses. Her boldness in seizing the lead seemed to mean that for the moment, he was satisfied for her to set the pace.

For a sizzling instant, her inexperience made her hang back. But she'd spent so long fantasizing about kissing Lord Shelburn that she let imagination feed into glorious reality.

She closed her eyes and experimented, seducing him with what she'd learned from his earth-shattering kisses. Kissing the corner of his mouth. Sucking his lower lip. Nipping. Circling his lips with her tongue.

She hovered in a tantalizing, enchanting space between play and fervor, but when he opened his mouth, desire overwhelmed her. She gave free rein to all her longing.

For a breathless interval, she sank into his sultry response. He met her demand with demands of his own and lashed his arms around her. She clung to the smooth, warm skin of those broad shoulders, as the world broke free from its moorings and went whirling into space.

If he could do this with a kiss, what on earth would he do when they shared that big bed?

Feeling dizzy, Kate drew back at last and struggled to focus on his face. She'd dreamed of his kisses, but the reality exceeded all those sentimental – and she now realized ignorant – yearnings.

The physical reality of being in Leighton's arms was so much more vivid than anything that her inadequate imagination could conjure up. Her virginal fancies dissolved under the powerful influence of actual seduction.

She felt so alive in his presence, more alive than she ever had before. As if someone had suddenly lit a lantern in a dark room. Already she knew that returning to darkness would leave her lost and forlorn.

"You're lovely," he murmured, stealing another quick kiss.

"Thank you." Nobody had ever called her lovely before. Most people called her formidable.

Leighton shifted back far enough to lift her leg and place one foot on his thigh. Earlier, he'd fumbled to untie his neckcloth, but now he made short work of unlacing her half boots.

When he placed a kiss on her instep, she gasped. She had no idea that her feet were so sensitive, but as he massaged the sole through her fine silk stocking, her toes curled in delight.

He regarded her with a glow in his eyes. "You like that?"

"I didn't know..."

He understood her incoherent attempt to explain and smiled so that her silly heart jumped about like a grasshopper in a lily bed. "Your whole body is a theater for pleasure. I look forward to showing you."

She gulped, speech deserting her yet again. The breath jammed anew in her throat, as he took his time untying her pink satin garter and rolling her stocking down her calf, then off her foot, leaving one leg bare to his touch.

He took his time discovering her, so that every inch between her knee and her toes warmed under the trailing fingers. With a leisurely enjoyment that left her shaking, he stroked her skin. Then he turned his attention to the other stocking.

Everywhere he touched made her burn and hunger. He built her aching need with slow, careful caresses.

When he tickled the skin behind her knee, she giggled. Although the Amazon of Bradbourne was a woman who never giggled.

But that redoubtable lady moved further and further out of reach with every minute Kate spent with Lord Shelburn. Right now, she was too enthralled to find that frightening.

Then her heart stopped altogether before it flung itself against her ribs in wild excitement. And nervous dread.

His hands had ventured under the lace edges of her drawers. His face was stark with intense concentration, and his eyelids lowered until thick black lashes hid those brilliant eyes. The marked black brows tilted down in what was almost a frown.

The loose pink garment left ample room for him to explore as far as her hips. As Kate's anticipation built, her breath emerged in audible gusts from between her parted lips.

When he stroked beneath the drawers, she'd closed her legs. Now he pushed the slippery material up and slid his hands along the inside of her thighs. With a sigh, she leaned back against the chair and let her legs fall open.

Leighton gave a muffled groan, as her change in position revealed the slit of her drawers. She closed her eyes, unable to watch as he drank in the sight of her intimate flesh.

"Lovely?" he murmured. "That doesn't do you justice."

With ruthless gentleness, Leighton parted her legs wider. She started when he placed a kiss on her mound. The idea of his mouth...*there* would frighten or disgust a decent woman, but Kate found the idea desperately exciting. Somewhere in the last few hours, she'd given up any claim to calling herself a decent woman.

Wanton blood seethed in her veins, as she wondered where else those brazen lips might stray. She waited in an agony of suspense, as he tugged at the strings tying her drawers around her waist.

When Kate dared to open her eyes, she found Leighton poised between her splayed legs. Her shift was scrunched around her midriff and her drawers sagged, revealing the pale plain of her stomach and the dark brown curls at the delta of her thighs. She looked altogether lost to sin.

The picture was so stirring and so shocking that she started to straighten.

"No, don't move."

If his words had held a trace of command, she might have broken free of the sensual bonds entangling her. But his voice was soft and husky and pleading, and his chiseled features were taut with a longing that she recognized because she felt its twin.

Even as a protest rose in her throat, it died unspoken. What Leighton did to her might be wicked, but it was also wonderful. So she reached out to stroke his bare chest in a silent gesture of compliance. And when he caught her hips in those hard capable hands and brought his head down between her legs, her cry expressed astonishment and pleasure, but no denial.

CHAPTER TEN

Kate had guessed what Leighton intended when he kissed her just above her sex. But nothing prepared her for the jolt of sensation when he buried his face in her cleft and began to torment her with his tongue and teeth.

"Leighton!" she cried out, as he tasted her most private places.

Her first reaction was to retreat, but the back of the chair kept her trapped. Nor, with him insinuated between her legs, could she close him out. Then all idea of resistance fled, as every nerve in her body bristled to sizzling life under his bold seduction.

When he concentrated on one particularly sensitive place, the turbulent throbbing intensified, then exploded in a wild conflagration. The rush of response had her quaking under his mouth and gasping, without ever seeming to inhale enough air to fill her lungs.

Shaking, she arched and slid down in the chair, widening the angle of her legs around him, while he continued to tease and pleasure her. Shaking hands buried in his thick dark hair, as she plunged off the edge of the world into a new, resplendent universe.

When a surge of liquid response marked the summit of her excitement, his low growl of encouragement vibrated through her sex in a way that only heightened her quivering rapture.

Lost in a storm of sensation, Kate released his head and curled her hands tight around the chair's arms. She needed something solid to hold onto. All the muscles in her body spasmed into ecstasy, as she panted under his wanton ministrations. Every time she thought that she reached her limit, he lifted her to greater heights.

After what felt like an eon of wicked delight, she drifted back to earth. She opened her eyes to find him contemplating her with that unfathomable dark gaze. His lips were full and satiny. His stare told her that he'd enjoyed what he'd done and even more, he'd enjoyed watching her lose control.

His eyes were black as night. She reminded herself that one could find one's way by the stars.

"I..." she began, before she realized that she had no idea what she wanted to say.

"What on earth was that?" "Thank you." "Can we do that again?"

Nothing seemed to fit the bill after Leighton had transported her to places that she'd never imagined existed.

"Is that your first climax?" He spoke as easily as if he offered his arm to help her over a puddle, instead of discussing the carnal tornado that had just swept her up into ecstasy.

"Is that what you call what just happened?" she asked, her voice husky. Ripples of sensation continued to flow through her body.

He shrugged as with unashamed relish, one hand wiped his lips. The taste of the most intimate parts of her body would linger. She still had trouble believing that he'd placed his mouth on her and summoned that momentous...*climax.*

"There are other words. Climax covers the occasion well enough."

Or no words at all. Kate was at a loss to explain what had happened. She'd had no idea that the body she'd possessed for thirty years was capable of such alchemy.

"Is that just because you kissed me...down there? Or is that what it's like when you take a woman to bed?"

Was it gauche to ask about what they'd done? At the very least, it should be embarrassing. But she was by nature curious, and this was the most interesting thing that had ever happened to her. Even more interesting than his kisses – and they'd been magnificent.

"I'm not a woman so I can't say, but if I do it right, yes, you'll climax again then." Leighton's lips turned down, as he sat back on his heels. While the position held a hint of subjugation, he looked as cocksure as ever. "Perhaps not the first time. I gather losing your virginity can be rather painful."

"Don't you know?"

He shrugged. "I steer clear of innocents – and innocents steer clear of me, if they have an ounce of sense. You know about my dreadful reputation."

Kate blushed, as she realized that her sprawled thighs hedged him in. Although after what had just happened, modesty was misplaced. After all, he'd examined her with unabashed interest when he'd undone her drawers, and since then, his tongue had explored every fold of her sex.

Nonetheless, she sat up. Although she only managed to bring her legs together, after Leighton slid back with a reluctance that pleased her.

"I'm an innocent," she said in a low voice.

Leighton sent her a searching look. "You're a virgin. I wouldn't say you're an innocent." Something in her blossomed, as his lips curled up with unashamed carnality. "Anyway, innocent or not, you're irresistible. You may be breaking a few of your own rules today, but so am I."

"I like to hear that."

His smile widened. "I thought you might. I'm encouraged by how fast you found your peak. I imagined that I'd have to work harder, but you melted in the most exquisite fashion."

Kate frowned, not sure if that was good. "I couldn't help it."

"I hope you can never help it. I adore knowing that the fire inside me matches the fire inside you."

Despite realizing that he praised her, nerves dried her mouth. He spoke with such confidence of using her body over and over. "When you touch me, I lose all contact with reality."

One eyebrow slanted upward. When he'd raised his head from between her legs, he looked like a sensual stranger. Now with every minute, he looked more like the worldly, sardonic rake. Not that the rake was much more than a stranger either.

"It's a privilege to show you what you've missed."

A saucy smile curled her lips – when she'd never given a man a saucy smile in her life. At the mill, her stern manner discouraged any disrespect. It was in so many ways an act. Today at last, she allowed someone to see her real self.

Good heavens, here she was, sitting half naked in front of a rake. The Bradbourne Amazon would give this new abandoned version of Kate Starr the cut direct.

"Perhaps it's time you showed me more." With a desperation that would have shocked the woman she was this morning, she thirsted to feel his hands on her breasts.

"I feel like I've corrupted you." Leighton's laugh held a hint of a crack, as he stared entranced at the flesh mounded above her spectacular corset.

Kate met his amused gaze. "Not yet."

He rose to his knees and drew her up for a kiss that ignited into an inferno. By the time he lifted his head, she was gasping and trembling.

"You make me mad," she whispered, although the hand she trailed down his chest conveyed more tenderness than passion, however passionate the kiss had been.

"I hope so." He stood with a smoothness that made her susceptible heart skip a beat. A vigorous, well-muscled male body was a glorious sight indeed. "Those undergarments are fiendishly attractive, but I'm agog to find out what's beneath them."

As she stood away from the chair, she smiled again. This afternoon, she seemed to be smiling a lot.

When her drawers drifted to the floor, she kicked them away. Her hands didn't shake, as she tugged the front fastenings of her corset open and shrugged the garment off. Leighton watched with unwavering attention and unmistakable approval.

He stepped forward and let his fingers wander down one shoulder to the rose satin ribbon that held her shift up. "Pretty."

She gulped, nerves returning. He was a breath away from stroking her breast. Even in her inexperience, she recognized that he teased her.

That wolfish smile was back. "Take it off."

He smiled a lot this afternoon, too. The anticipation in his expression made her knees go weak. That, and the fact that without her shift, she'd be naked. Not that the diaphanous silk left much to the imagination.

But if Kate meant to do this wild, dangerous, disreputable thing, she needed to be brave. So she raised her chin again, not in defiance of Leighton, but in defiance of the forces of convention and upbringing and morality. Her hands remained steady as she caught the slippery material and tugged it over her head.

She dropped her shift. Although the room was warm, the air felt cold on her skin and gave her goose bumps. More nerves, she suspected.

It took every ounce of willpower to meet Leighton's gaze. She braced to discover triumph or greed or hunger. When she read wonder in that striking face, her heart performed another dizzying flip.

She was beautiful.

Shelburn had recognized that from the beginning, but this unveiling of Kate Starr's nakedness took his breath away. She was just right. Strong. Shapely. Designed to fit his hands.

Even more powerful was the knowledge that he was the only man she'd trusted enough to share all this loveliness.

A woman's nudity hadn't rendered him speechless since his first encounters with the fair sex when he was a youth. But something about the elegant lines and curves of Kate's form made his jaded heart skip a beat. Then another. Then another. Until his head swam and his soul ached.

"Please say something," she stammered, hands hovering in front of her breasts and sex as the silence lengthened. She wasn't trying to shield herself from his view, but he could tell that she wanted to. Perhaps part of what made this moment so poignant was her beguiling mixture of bashfulness and pride.

Unprecedented, disturbing, to find himself tongue-tied. None of his former liaisons had prepared him for this brief affair, not least that Kate kept catching the practiced debauchee out and slicing away all his old, tired stratagems.

It hurt to force an answer out of his constricted throat. "You're perfect."

The words were damnably inadequate. He, the gentleman renowned for his smooth, seductive tongue, sounded as awkward as an untaught rustic.

Shelburn struggled to come up with a compliment worthy of Kate and of the renowned voluptuary that he was. But try as he might, his reeling mind couldn't muster the hackneyed phrases that he'd used so often before.

His hands curled at his sides, as they itched to discover that smooth white flesh. But he was too busy taking in every delectable detail to think of closing the distance between them just yet.

He drank in the straight shoulders, their tense line betraying courage and vulnerability. His attention lowered to the firm, high breasts, with their puckered coffee-colored nipples. She was all woman, with the generosity to offer a man a soft landing, yet the strength to remind him that this was no silly, untried girl.

His gaze traced the sinuous dip and flare of waist and hips, down to the long, graceful legs. Yet again, he admired their lithe shape and her neat, narrow feet.

As his heart galloped, he licked his lips. He'd never forget the salty taste of her ecstasy, as she writhed under his mouth. Yet that was only a hint of the heaven awaiting with this woman. He promised himself that before the night was out, he'd kiss every inch of Kate Starr, from those pale toes up to the ruffled crown of her dark head.

Color lined her strong cheekbones as his inspection continued. She drew that thick fall of hair forward, until it cascaded in lush waves over her breasts.

If she hoped to restore some modesty, she wasted her time. The curtain of deep, silky brown made Shelburn more aware than ever of the creamy flesh beneath. She was Eve in the Garden of Eden. Pure female, offering herself to the fortunate male.

"Perhaps...perhaps you should take off your breeches," she said hesitantly.

He liked that she was bold enough to express what she wanted. But in this case, he meant to deny her.

He gestured at his one remaining garment. "If I'm naked, you'll find yourself under me before you can say 'not yet.'"

Those serious hazel eyes didn't shift from his face. "I might say 'yes, please.'"

For a long moment, Shelburn stared at her in shock, then without being aware that he moved, she was in his arms. He kissed that hot, clever mouth with a voracious hunger that beggared his experience, however vast.

Kate met him without hesitation. Difficult to believe that she'd never shared a real kiss until today. This was a woman born to hold him in thrall.

His hands discovered the warm satin of her skin, traced that straight, stubborn spine, kneaded the firm flesh of her buttocks, until she moaned into his mouth and plastered herself to his chest.

With eager urgency, he turned her until the curve of her rump nestled into his groin. The blast of heat through his breeches made him press forward. Breathing in great gusts, he buried his face in her hair. He drank in her evocative scent and knew that ever after, all other air would prove an inadequate substitute.

At last, at last, he cupped her breasts. She jerked at the contact, before leaning back. When he squeezed the opulent flesh and his thumbs brushed those impudent nipples, a broken cry escaped her.

He raised his head from the luxuriant mass of hair and peered over her shoulder to watch his hands toy with her breasts. Tanned and hard and purposeful on her alabaster skin.

Still teasing one nipple, he slid his other hand down her flat stomach. Kate trembled beneath the seeking caress. A seeking caress that held an unsettling hint of possession.

Shelburn never made claims on a woman, beyond the lure of pleasure. But as he traced the hard line of Kate's ribs and the soft plain of her belly, his pulse pounded out one word over and over. *Mine. Mine. Mine.*

He raked his fingers through the damp, silky nest of curls below her stomach, then slid his hand between her legs to the sleek folds that his mouth had already explored. As his finger and thumb pinched her nipple, he teased the entrance to her body.

She stiffened in surprise, then when he began to stroke in and out, he heard a long exhalation of surrender. She tilted her head back against his shoulder and bumped her hips forward in silent encouragement.

He rubbed her clitoris until she was shaking and moaning. She slumped against him, as though her very bones dissolved.

Shelburn had never known a woman so responsive. When he took her to bed, she'd blaze into pure flame. Kate mightn't be sexually experienced, but the passion that she contained left him in awe. And lost to desire.

As his thumb stimulated her most sensitive place, he felt her tumble over into another climax. A broken moan emerged from her throat. As she sagged, her muscles spasmed around his fingers.

His finger lingered inside her, while the small internal earthquakes receded. He brushed aside her hair and scraped his teeth along the nerve running down her neck to her shoulder. On an incoherent mutter of delight, she tightened.

He muffled a groan against her skin and squeezed her breast again. She felt like heaven in his arms.

"That was...wonderful," Kate said in a broken voice that didn't sound at all like the serene lady who had joined him in the race.

Some instinct told Shelburn that she revealed a secret self. Not just because she was sumptuously naked, but because the woman who thrilled to his lightest caress abandoned all defenses. She threw herself headlong into the pursuit of rapture.

"*You're* wonderful," he murmured in reply, as he slipped his hand free and caught her hips. When his erect cock rubbed against her buttocks, he closed his eyes and fought the pounding ache in his balls.

She turned in his arms to regard him with heavy eyes. "Take me to bed, Leighton. I'm ready."

He hoped to hell she was. He wasn't sure how much more he could withstand without spilling in his breeches.

In society's less respectable circles, his control with a woman was legendary. He could excite a lover for hours without seeking his own release.

Kate turned that reputation on its head. He wanted her so much, he wasn't even confident that he'd make it onto the sheets. Only the knowledge that this was her first time and he wanted to make it good for her kept his urges leashed.

He pulled far enough away to take one of her hands and kiss it. He couldn't stop touching her. She was as addictive as opium. Tenderness wasn't his language, but he couldn't deny the tenderness he felt as her gaze softened on him.

"Then come with me, my darling," he said softly.

"Don't call me that." To his surprise, the endearment made her frown. "You don't have to."

"I want to."

She rose on her toes and kissed him on the lips with a clumsy enthusiasm that was more devastating than a kiss from any of his society paramours. Perhaps because Kate's kiss conveyed a world of ardent sincerity.

Shelburn wouldn't have said that he dealt in sincerity, either. But with Kate, sincerity turned out to be as inescapable as bullets on a battlefield.

Just as he got into the spirit of things, she drew away. "Call me Kate. Then I'm sure that you remember who shares your bed. I know I'm not special, but for today I'd like to pretend I am."

It was his turn to frown. "Kate—"

"Yes, that's just what I want to hear." She kissed him again, before he could argue with her unflattering assessment. Which was insane when this affair, like all his affairs, was entirely a matter of physical enjoyment. If a lover sought something more than a hot tumble with no promises, she needed to look elsewhere.

Hadn't he made that clear to Kate earlier? She merely followed the rules that he'd laid down.

Absurd to resent her cooperation. He'd told her that he was no prince, and she'd believed him. Too late to wish that she preserved one or two of her foolish illusions.

By the time she finished kissing him, his head was spinning. He struggled to string the words together to insist that he didn't take this encounter in his stride. He knew the importance of what she gave him, and he valued that gift more than anything else he could remember in his gilded existence.

But she was drawing him toward the bedroom door. He was in a lather to bury his dick deep inside her. When a naked woman he wanted like the very devil led him up to the gates of paradise, reason proved elusive.

Shelburn had things that he needed to talk to Kate about. Essential things.

But he'd been burning up for her all day, and holding back while she'd found her peak twice had left him in agony. The time for talk had passed. The time for touch and passion and two bodies uniting in the ancient dance of mating had arrived.

He'd entered into this affair, sure that he'd remain in charge, as he always did. Now the notorious rake swallowed to shift a lump of unfamiliar emotion from his throat, before he let the untried virgin guide him into the bedchamber.

CHAPTER ELEVEN

*T*wice now, Leighton had transported Kate to heaven and back. A sultry, tumultuous, radiant heaven that she'd had no idea existed.

The words to describe that plunge into fire continued to elude her. A fire that blazed with pleasure and left her quaking and exhausted and drifting in a blissful haze afterward.

But he was yet to find release, and the strain was showing. The skin clung to the bones of his face, and he looked drawn and on edge.

She, too, hungered for the ultimate joining. He'd invited her into a new world of sensation, but each time she tumbled over the precipice into ecstasy, she'd felt empty and strangely alone.

For too much of her life, she'd been alone. Ever since Sylvie and her parents had died. Today was the first time in years when she relaxed the self-control that ruled her. Only now did she recognize how lonely her life had been in recent years.

She stopped on the rug in the center of the room and turned to Leighton. Because it was afternoon, her shocking behavior seemed even more shocking. Such sins belonged under cover of night.

Summoning every morsel of courage, she ran her hands down his bare chest. His skin was warm and smooth under her touch, and she felt the flex of hard muscle, as she lingered on his pectorals and traced the line of his sternum.

Leighton quivered under her hesitant investigation, and she was close enough to hear his breath catch and to see his Adam's apple bob as he swallowed. Encouraged by these signs that her tentative caresses stirred him, she moved closer to taste him. A hint of salt and something musky that she guessed was male arousal. She kissed his chest again and filled her lungs with his piquant scent.

A soft rumble emerged from deep in his throat. A hint of protest. A growl of approval.

His male parts filled the front of his breeches. This visible proof of his desire excited her, even as apprehension churned in her stomach when she imagined what was about to happen.

Her hands slid lower, his hair a soft prickle against her palms. She had no idea that a man's body would prove so fascinating. Curiosity brought her to the waistband of his breeches. She bit her lip in concentration, as she worked out the arrangement of buttons.

When at last she released the front fall, he shuddered. A murmur of awe escaped her at the sight of his male member swelling against a single layer of material.

"Have you ever seen a naked man before?"

She shook her head, working at the last buttons. "I've seen etchings of statues."

Tension roughened his laugh. "Most of the time, they're not rampant."

"Is that the word?" she asked faintly.

Until now, her hands had been steady. As she brushed aside the final fold of buckskin, they trembled, despite her best efforts to appear calm.

Although Kate wasn't looking at his face, she heard a smile in his voice. "I'm doing wonders for your vocabulary."

"I'm very grateful," she muttered, which elicited a grunt of amusement.

At last, she saw his male parts. She suspected that her vocabulary, however extended, lacked an adequate term for his sexual organ. Every word that she knew held an unappealing hint of the clinical.

Seeing Leighton's rod for the first time made her feel anything but clinical. She swallowed to moisten a mouth that had gone as dry as the Sahara. Her hands retreated from his breeches to curl at her sides.

"Are you horrified?" Even through her overwhelming wonder, she heard the worried note in his question. "I'm a blasted big bugger. It's one of the reasons that I kept my breeches on. I didn't want you swooning away in maidenly dread."

"I'm not swooning," she said, her neutral tone altogether manufactured.

"You're not saying very much."

"I'm..."

"Disgusted? Terrified?"

It was an effort to drag her attention away from that hard column of flesh, emerging from the nest of black hair between his legs. Had she called his body fascinating? She'd had no idea.

"Impressed."

She realized that he'd been genuinely unsure about her reaction, because she couldn't mistake the relief flooding his features. By nature candid, she went on. "And a little daunted."

"A little" was a huge understatement.

That part of him would soon penetrate her untried body. For the life of her, she couldn't imagine how he'd fit.

But Leighton didn't seem to have any doubts on that account, and she bowed to his greater knowledge. After all, who would have thought that a man's mouth between her legs could conjure the greatest joy she'd ever known?

Kate presumed that he'd managed to insert his huge member into all the other ladies he'd serviced over the years. The evidence of her eyes must be misleading.

"All this just means I want you."

She extended one hand toward him. "May I touch you?"

As he caught her wrist, his laugh was strained. "Later."

That seemed odd when his hand on her sex had summoned the most magical responses. "It's not pleasurable?"

Another cracked laugh. "It's too pleasurable. I'm in a fever to be inside you. I fear that even the briefest brush of your hand would unman me."

Kate was glad to hear that he was also at the mercy of this searing attraction. She wanted him mad for her.

He released her and pushed his gaping breeches down his slim hips. A few fumbling movements – another betrayal of how his control frayed, because he was in general a deft man – and he stood before her without a stitch of clothing.

Her eyes rounded. "Good heavens," she breathed, licking her lips as excitement surged like a rising tide. "You're magnificent."

He was. In expensive tailoring, Leighton was superb. Naked, he verged on the godlike. Tall. Perfect proportions. Weighted with muscles that made even a Long Meg like Kate feel ridiculously female and delicate.

Her avid gaze settled on his virility once again. Her hands curled even tighter at her sides, as they itched to hold all that potency.

"What a lot of nonsense." He reacted to her compliment with charming bashfulness, which set her already overburdened heart twisting about inside her chest like a landed trout. "I'm not magnificent. You are."

She cast him a quick laughing glance, even as his praise answered her longing for him to find her as beautiful as she found him. "Let's settle the argument by saying we're both magnificent."

The delight that filled his face did more silly things to her heart. Perhaps it was lucky that he seized her up before she could dwell on just what those silly feelings meant. He kissed her with a ruthless fervor that made her quiver with longing.

Pressed so close, she felt every aroused inch. A choked murmur of anticipation rose from her throat, before the world reeled as he lifted her high. When he cradled her in his arms as though she were as light as thistledown, something hard and controlled inside her melted in feminine surrender.

He carried her across to the bed so easily that she didn't feel like the Amazon of Bradbourne, who was too tall and too strong and altogether too much like a man. Instead, she became a responsive, generous woman, who gave her chosen lover everything he needed.

It was a glorious feeling. Almost as glorious as the sensations that Leighton had created when he'd touched her between the legs.

This desire had restored something significant that the years playing the canny mill owner had stolen. Perhaps the knowledge that she was a woman with feelings and needs and more to give the world than a tidy list of pounds, shillings, and pence earned.

Whatever happened after this – and enough of her pragmatic self remained for her to recognize that she and Leighton must part, once they'd sated their appetites – that knowledge would linger. This seduction provided her with a priceless and enduring gift.

So when he swept back the bedcovers and set her on the sheets as if she was made of Venetian glass, Kate brought him down for more kisses.

"Kate, I'm not sure I can wait."

The craving she heard stoked her arousal to a conflagration. Her legs parted, leaving him poised between her thighs.

She nipped at his lips, speaking in a jerky pattern between kisses. "Don't...wait. I want...you. I want you so...much."

He groaned and propped himself up on his elbows. As he stared at her, his eyes glittered, and a flush marked his spectacular cheekbones. She'd always thought that he was extraordinarily attractive. Right now, with every atom of his being concentrated on her, his male beauty stole her breath.

Speech became impossible. So Kate tilted her hips in a silent plea for him to end her torment. Her grip on his back tightened. She felt his muscles contract, as he drew back then surged forward.

Despite her earlier climaxes, her body stretched to the point of pain. She'd been right to fear his size. She gasped with stunned discomfort and dug her nails into his skin.

He pressed deeper. A sharp, tearing sensation made her curl toward him. Then he went still, his throbbing weight within her proclaiming her as his.

The act's intimacy astonished her. She felt his every breath. Leighton had become part of her.

He stared down at her, his gaze questioning.

"I'm fine," she said in a strangled voice, her grip on his shoulders bruising.

A faint smile curved his lips. "It doesn't sound like it."

"It's just...unexpected," she said, wriggling further into the bed.

"Awful?"

"No."

"Liar."

"No, it really isn't awful." In fact, it became less awful by the second. The change of position eased her frantic hold. "It hurt a little at first, but we knew it would."

His brows drew together. "I don't like hurting you."

He rose higher on his elbows. Again the movement lessened her discomfort. Kate could almost say that the intrusion began to feel natural.

"I'll live."

"I hope so."

"That's nice to hear."

When he adjusted his hips, an almost pleasurable frisson caught her unawares. The act had forced all the breath from her. Now her lungs filled, and her agonizing tension relaxed. With that, her secret places embraced the hard reality of a man's possession.

Faint humor lit his eyes to dark starlight. "How on earth would I explain a dead body to Mr. Fletcher? It would be deuced inconvenient."

To her surprise, she laughed. A strange sensation with a man inside her. Her muscles smoothed around him, and the brief pain receded to a memory. Her hands loosened, and she stroked those broad, sinewy shoulders. "I wouldn't like to trouble you."

"So kind. Lift your knees."

Kate obeyed. "Oh!"

His smile intensified. "Better?"

"Yes." After the awkward beginning, she'd been pleased when it no longer hurt to contain him. But with this latest shift, a bolt of sensation that didn't feel a thousand miles away from the stirrings of a climax blasted her.

Leighton regarded her as though she was the most fascinating object in the universe. "Shall we try for more?"

This time, she didn't have to pretend enthusiasm. "I'd like that."

She waited for him to move, but he lingered to kiss her. The fierce pressure of his lips told her that his control cost more than he admitted. He might sound calm and ironic and composed, but his kiss expressed a thirst for release that was as exciting as his touch.

Kate tangled her hands in his thick black hair and drew him near for another kiss, then bumped up in a way that she couldn't imagine doing when he started. The tight fit no longer felt like invasion. It felt like perfect union.

Instead of pulling back, he settled more firmly, then moved his hips in a subtle circle. Response rushed through her, stronger this time. She curled her fingers around his hard biceps. "Do that again."

"With pleasure."

This time, the action was more deliberate and she saw stars. "Oh, Leighton, that's…"

"Hold on to me." His voice was warm with satisfaction.

She linked her hands at his nape. Silky curls tickled her fingers.

He tightened his hips and withdrew with such languor that she had time to feel every inch of that impressive appendage. As he slid free, her body clung and all her nerves went on alert to the surge of pleasure.

"That's...so good," she panted, tugging at his hair.

He pushed forward. This time, she accepted him with a welcome that astounded her. No pain. No difficulty. Leighton fitted inside her, as if they'd been created to join together.

The physical response was overwhelming. To her dismay, the emotional response was even more ungovernable. As he seated himself deep, she felt like she'd traveled full circle. The beautiful boy she'd fallen in love with was now the ardent man who owned her body and soul.

Somehow it seemed fated.

Stop it, Kate.

For pity's sake, she couldn't let herself think that way. Nothing but heartbreak extended ahead, if she wallowed in idiotic romantic fantasies.

But her hands were loving as they glided down that long back to his tight buttocks. When she kissed him, tenderness melded with ardor.

This time, his withdrawal was swifter and he thrust into her with more vigor. Her blood pumped harder with every plunge, and soon she felt the now familiar rise toward ecstasy. Astounding how fast discomfort transformed into pleasure. She dug her fingers into those firm cheeks and squirmed in wordless encouragement for him to continue.

As they strove toward the peak, they both breathed in erratic gusts. Leighton's movements became choppy, less controlled, as her responses spiraled higher. When she arched, he reached a place inside her that sent rivers of light rushing along her veins.

"Oh, yes..." she said on a broken sigh and pressed closer. His next thrust stimulated that astonishing space, sending her crashing through into blinding delight.

He buried his face in her shoulder, and his teeth scraped her shoulder. The sharpness only added to the glorious torrents engulfing her.

Through her volcanic climax, she felt him go rigid. He wrenched free of her body and spilled on her bare stomach in a hot splatter of effortful release.

Kate was still shaking with pleasure, when he rolled to the side and slumped facedown into the pillows beside her.

CHAPTER TWELVE

Shaking and gasping, Shelburn stretched out beside Kate and waited for the raging tumult in his blood to settle. Beside him, she lay silent, although he could hear the faint uneven hiss of her breath as she drifted down from what he knew had been a mighty orgasm.

A vast, empty chasm opened inside him when, by God, he should be elated. He'd shown his lover a world of vivid pleasure. She'd been a goddess in his arms. Yet....

Yet...

He always used withdrawal to avoid consequences. It had never before felt wrong to spill outside a woman. But with Kate, it undoubtedly did.

He had no idea why. But he loathed this grim hopelessness that gripped him.

Even more puzzling, this dismal reaction came after an encounter that had granted unrivaled pleasure, despite all his naughty games over the years. Kate had accepted him with a melting sweetness that had made him feel clean and pure. When even as a boy, he couldn't remember feeling clean and pure.

If anyone had said that he'd bask in an innocence as foreign to him as far Cathay, he'd have scoffed. But that explosion of passion had shattered his cynical shell. Had proven, in fact, that his cynicism was a shell and not bone-deep reality.

This affair that had promised an amusing diversion in London became more damned complicated by the minute. And Leighton Anstey didn't do complicated.

Self-preservation urged him to run for the hills. But to his chagrin, having tasted the incomparable joys of being inside Kate Starr, he couldn't summon the will to run anywhere. Until he had to. Despite his troubling reaction to what they'd just done in this bed.

As his breathing eased and he kept his eyes closed in a futile attempt to avoid looking square at his dilemma, he tried to tell himself that nothing so very special had just happened. Yes, Kate had been untouched and she'd surrendered her virginity with a generosity that slashed a rift across his well-protected heart. And, yes, once she'd accustomed herself to him, her responsiveness had been a miracle. And, yes, Shelburn had veered perilously close to filling her with his seed.

But none of those things needed to change him or his life.

Such an irresistible new lover left him on edge. That was the obvious explanation. There was no reason for this unaccustomed soul-searching. Kate didn't live by the same rules as he and his worldly paramours did. Not to mention that some old certainties had cracked when he'd watched Verena find love, whereas once he'd have sworn that she was as hardened and sophisticated as he was.

There was no reason to worry. No reason at all.

He'd stay with Kate long enough to work through this powerful but temporary fascination. Once the novelty wore off, he'd return to playing the heartless rake. As he'd so enjoyed playing the heartless rake all his adult life. He'd leave this room with a raft of delightful memories, while Kate Starr would toddle back to her real life, equipped with a thorough education in the carnal arts.

Everything was as it should be.

In the meantime, he and Kate would partake of a banquet of sensual pleasure.

His disquiet subsided, and he prepared to roll over and inform the lady that she was lovely and marvelous and a dream to hold in his arms. All the nonsense that he spouted, once he'd used a woman.

Shelburn squashed the reluctant perception that when he paid Kate those stale compliments, they wouldn't be stale at all. That idea was just another symptom of his strange humor.

Before he could shift, he felt the weight of her hand on his shoulder. She reached across to establish a contact that he'd been woefully slow to make. Devil take him, this fit of the megrims was unforgivable. After her first time with a man, he owed her reassurance at the very least.

But her touch didn't feel like a rebuke, or even like a demand. It felt like...*connection.*

It stopped his breath. Damn it, it stopped his very heart.

Instead of an imposition, her hand on his skin felt like a blessing. A confirmation that their tempestuous union had been more than just another fuck.

All Shelburn's specious arguments against admitting that what had just happened was unprecedented and burdened with unforeseen consequence dissolved into thin air.

Bloody, bloody hell, he was in trouble here. And he had no idea what to do about it.

When Kate touched Leighton's shoulder, he went rigid. Before she could pull back, he relaxed under her palm like a half-wild cat willing to accept a moment's fondling.

The contact helped settle the turmoil raging inside her. She sucked in a broken breath and stared up at the heavy oak beams crossing the plaster ceiling.

What an afternoon it had been. She didn't feel at all like the person who had arrived in London this morning, resigned to a future that made sense in every way except the ways her heart wanted.

After that shattering intimacy, she'd needed to confirm her link with her lover. She had no idea of the etiquette for this occasion. How could she? But she'd imagined that after sexual relations, lovers might lie entwined in a gentle aftermath. Having shared such transcendent pleasure, wouldn't they want to extend the closeness as long as they could?

But the end of her first experience of lovemaking had been Leighton's violent withdrawal, followed by his gasping release on her stomach. Then he'd rolled away to lie unmoving beside her.

No words. No kisses. No cuddles.

Perhaps her disappointment wasn't justified. But she was disappointed all the same. Kate hadn't felt lonely when his body moved in hers. She felt heartbreakingly lonely now.

As the silence extended, insecurities rose up like starving rats and started to gnaw at her.

He'd wanted her. She couldn't have mistaken that. And she was sure that he'd enjoyed what they'd done. At least at first. He'd seemed on fire to have her.

But perhaps in the end, she'd let him down. What else could explain this awkward hiatus?

Odd that she felt more at sea now than she'd felt during their prickly, flirtatious negotiations before the act. The virgin had possessed a confidence that her now ruined self altogether lacked.

The mess on her stomach was sticky. She should get up and clean it off. She was damp and swollen between the legs, too, and a little sore, although pleasure had soon banished the pain from his penetration. When she joined him in the bed, she hadn't felt cheap or used. Whereas right now, she felt rather low.

With a muffled sigh, she lifted her hand from his back and sat up to swing her legs over the side of the bed. She winced as the movement raised a protest from muscles that she hadn't known she possessed.

Earlier, her nakedness had seemed daring. Now she wished her dress was near at hand, instead of in the other room.

Not that Leighton showed the slightest interest in her body. He was yet to glance in her direction.

"What are you doing?" he asked behind her in a husky voice.

She didn't turn her head. "I need a wash." She struggled to keep her voice even.

What was the point of sulking? This man didn't owe her anything. If he'd decided that he'd mistaken the extent of his attraction, that was his right.

He caught the arm that she braced against the rumpled sheets. "Don't go."

Kate wanted to shake off his grip. She really did. Her pride insisted upon it. But it seemed that her earlier enchantment hadn't altogether forsaken her, because she didn't break free.

"Let me wash you," he murmured, when she neither answered nor moved out of reach.

"I don't think I want to stay here." She hated how emotion thickened her voice.

She'd like to pretend that what they'd done hadn't affected her beyond physical pleasure. It would be the ultimate humiliation should Leighton decide to give her another lecture about romantic illusions.

His hand slid down to her wrist in what felt like a caress. "I'm sorry."

While something told her that he didn't apologize very often, the thought didn't mollify her hurt feelings. She still didn't look at him. "For taking me to bed?"

"Damn it, Kate." The bed moved behind her, as he released her arm and shifted.

All of a sudden, he was pressed against her back and his legs rested on either side of hers. "I'm an idiot. I'm a dolt. I'm the lowest swine in creation. But never think that I regret what we just did."

She stiffened, but although the arms he curled around her were loose, she couldn't quite summon the will to reject him.

"Why shouldn't I think that?" She wasn't doing a very good job of hiding her pique.

He sighed, and she felt him bury his face in her tangled hair. "You took me by surprise."

"I'm so sorry I wasn't up to your usual standard," she said with a hint of acid. More than a hint, if she was honest. "If only I'd told you I was a virgin. Oh, that's right. I did."

His arms tightened before he let her go. She tried not to mind.

She stared down into her lap. She wasn't a woman who cried, no matter how unhappy she was. But she had a suspicion that if she caught sight of the man who had broken her heart, she'd start bawling like a lost calf.

That was the problem with dismantling one's defenses. There was nothing left to protect one when attacks came. Most of all from unexpected directions.

The bed shifted again. She didn't look up, until she realized that he was standing in front of her.

He'd pulled on his breeches, which made her feel lower than ever. She grabbed a pillow and pressed it to her breasts. It wasn't the most elegant covering and the mess on her stomach would stain the pillowcase, but it hid her between her neck and the top of her thighs. She couldn't bear to sit in front of him, abject and naked.

She peered up, daring him to laugh at her. But he looked stricken and not at all like the sophisticate that he presented to the world. He also looked at a complete loss. She imagined that being at a disadvantage with a woman was an even rarer occurrence for the noble Earl of Shelburn than apologizing.

"You're misunderstanding. Deliberately, I can't help thinking." He paused. "But you have a right to be angry. I should have taken you in my arms and told you how superb you are. I should have kissed you and praised you. I know that, and I can only apologize again."

"I'm not a child," Kate said in a cold tone, although she had a nasty feeling that perhaps she was behaving like one. "You don't need to give me a bonbon and pat me on the head and tell me I did a good job with my arithmetic."

"It was your first sexual experience." His lips flattened. Not in a smile. "You had a call on my tenderness and gratitude, if nothing else."

Her eyes narrowed. "So why didn't I get it?"

As always his bashfulness was disarming. She struggled to harden her heart against him.

"I've had many lovers."

"I know that. You don't need to give me the details."

"I'm not boasting." He made a sweeping gesture. "I'm trying to explain why I acted like such a blockhead, after you were so magnificent."

Surprise and gratification forceful enough to worry her set her mind whirling. *Magnificent?* He'd called her that before, but even so, she was astonished.

Some of her pique faded. And her injured feelings. "Magnificent" didn't sound like he'd hated holding her in his arms.

Kate licked her lips and forced herself to speak through a tight throat. She'd told herself over and over that she was nothing special. If she thought she was, she asked for trouble. But what else was Leighton saying now than that their encounter had taken him into new territory?

"You'll have to be clear. I'm not worldly enough to read between the lines."

"I...I found myself utterly overcome."

Her puzzlement increased. "Because I was a virgin?"

He'd said that he didn't deal with innocents.

Leighton shook his head and a self-deprecating smile curved his lips, although he continued to look on edge and unhappy. "Because you're you."

"I don't understand." Although she could see that she'd been wrong thinking he'd decided she wasn't worth his trouble.

"I'm not sure that I do either. I gave you every drop of myself and still I wanted to give you more. I almost forgot to withdraw, I was so lost to what I felt in your arms. I *never* forget to withdraw. For the first time, I found myself at the mercy of unparalleled pleasure. I'm not explaining this very well."

She clutched the pillow closer, in part because she feared that her leaping heart might crash right through her ribs. "That doesn't always happen?"

He shook his head with a vehemence that she couldn't mistake. "I'm a disgrace to the fraternity of rakes."

He didn't sound pleased about it. That, most of all, convinced her that he was sincere.

Kate responded in the crisp tone that always got her swift obedience at the mill. "I wouldn't say that."

He must know that she was on the verge of relenting. How could she help it, when he said such unexpected, wonderful things?

"Don't go, Kate." His voice deepened to a velvety persuasion that turned her blood to syrup. It was terrifying how susceptible she was. "Stay and let me be the lover you've dreamed of. We've just started. I promise that I'll try and get a better grip on my reactions."

She studied him, troubled and curious and flattered. Every instinct told her that like her, he struggled to make sense of this overwhelming attraction. But she'd entered an unfamiliar world today, and she couldn't be sure of the rules. He might give this speech to every lady he seduced.

Except that his self-disgust was clear. And his discomfort with the realms that he ventured into.

Perhaps she wasn't alone in discovering something new and powerful today.

One thing that she'd discovered was quite how vulnerable she was. Leighton had the capacity to devastate her. The wisest choice would be to stick to her decision and go.

Wisdom, it seemed, wasn't to prevail. As she stared into that remarkable face, her frantic grip on the pillow eased. "You could...you could still do some of those things you mentioned."

"Yes?"

"You could hold me and kiss me and tell me that I'm wonderful," she said in a small voice.

His face contracted with what she couldn't help but read as tenderness. And a relief so mighty that it made her stomach clench in response. Astonishing as it was to realize, he'd dreaded her leaving him.

She'd come to Leighton's bed with few qualms about surrendering her chastity. Yet now, it took a major effort of will to lift the pillow away and drop it to the floor. Once she was naked to his view, she itched to grab her protection back again.

The appreciation that lit his eyes soothed her embarrassment. He stepped forward and tilted her face for a gentle kiss. "You're wonderful. I cherish you. I'm honored that you came to my bed. You transported me to heaven."

"That's a start."

"When I hold you close, the world becomes a new and better place." As he stared down at her with an admiration that went a long way toward smoothing her ruffled feathers, his smile looked almost natural. "You're a glorious lover."

She didn't return his smile. "No need to overdo it."

"It's true."

"Hmm."

She could see that he didn't like her skepticism. He kissed her again and after a moment's resistance, she kissed him back with a longing that had only strengthened since he'd taken her.

He raised his head and smiled, as if she truly was as wonderful as he'd said. "Lie down, and I'll wash you. You must be uncomfortable."

He was right. She felt sticky and out of sorts, and that kiss had reminded her how much she enjoyed his touch. So she stretched out on the untidy bedclothes and watched as he crossed to the screen that hid the washstand.

She heard soft splashing. He must be washing before he came back to her.

"The water's lukewarm, I'm afraid," he said, sounding more like himself. He'd sounded so very shaken when he tried to explain his reaction to possessing her.

"I don't mind."

The servants had brought hot water and clean towels when they tidied away the meal. But that was quite a while ago.

Leighton appeared from behind the screen, carrying a bowl and with a couple of white linen towels draped over his arm.

Now that her swirling uncertainty receded, Kate took the chance to note what a striking picture the earl made in the last of the afternoon light. The sun through the open window edged him in gold, so he looked like a gilded statue from a cathedral. She had a sudden poignant memory of calling him a medieval knight all those years ago at Rushby Hall.

Then her gaze snagged on the marks scoring his burnished skin. She frowned. "I scratched you."

"War wounds."

His dry response prompted a huff of amusement. It was a relief to revert to ironic humor.

For a while there, Kate had poised on the brink of an abyss of emotion. The sensation had made her dizzy, and terrified that if she lost her balance, she'd never find it again. Leighton wasn't the only one unwilling to plumb the depths of the feeling that extended between them.

"I'm sorry."

"Don't be." He cast a careless glance at the marks on his arms. "It was exciting."

Exciting? High praise from such an experienced man.

He set the bowl on the nightstand and took a flannel out of the water. He wrung it out and placed it on her stomach. At the first touch of the damp cloth on her skin, she sighed with pleasure.

He swept the flannel across her skin to rinse away the remaining traces of his seed. "Not too cold?"

"No, it's nice. Refreshing."

As he washed her breasts and arms and legs, he was quiet. She drifted between half-dozing and observing him. His expression was serious, as if he undertook a vitally important task.

Was she wrong to feel that his care contained a touch of worship? She was trying her best to stay sensible, but he didn't make it easy.

"Spread your legs," he murmured.

The impulse to say something saucy in response crossed her mind, but the gentle mood was balm to her soul, so she obeyed without a word.

He'd been gentle since he'd started washing her. Now he was so careful, he threatened to break her heart.

He soothed the swollen flesh between her legs with cool water and a tender hand. "Are you sore?"

"No." Her body felt like it had been through a major change, but she wasn't in pain.

"I'm glad."

Leighton washed and dried her with a thorough sweetness that melted the last of her resentment. He lingered on her cleft, and the beginnings of arousal sliced through the languorous mood. She'd imagined after she'd scaled such heights the first time, that she wouldn't be able to muster any interest in amorous play for quite a while.

She'd imagined wrongly.

As the cloth stimulated that hidden place, she moved against the sheets with a faint murmur of complaint. He met her gaze as she caught his wrist, feeling the strong bones and muscles beneath his skin.

She didn't know what he saw in her eyes, but his expression changed from solicitous care to heated focus. He lifted the cloth away. "Kate?"

Just her name on a rising inflection, but she knew what he was asking.

"Show me more," she whispered.

While he'd tended to her, his features had softened. Now they hardened with masculine intent.

He dropped the flannel into the bowl and bent to place a kiss below her navel. Her skin tingled beneath his lips. Kate waited for him to move lower and kiss her sex again.

She was rather disgruntled, when he raised his head and studied her with a penetrating gaze. "Are you sure you're ready? I can wait until you've recovered. I'm not a barbarian."

He wasn't. She discovered instead that he was a considerate lover. Apart from those moments when his response to taking her had left him so shaken – and how she could she blame him for that?

"I'm sure." Then more daring, "I want to."

When his eyes flared, she prepared for him to seize her. But he turned away to pick up the bowl and crumpled towels. He strode across the room and left them behind the screen. Then he returned to stand by the bed and tug off his breeches. In his haste, he was all thumbs. She smiled at this proof that he wanted her, too.

Kate pushed up against the pillows to get a better view. Her blatant curiosity made his member swell. The sight excited her – now she knew just where all these disturbing feelings led.

Heat flooded her, making her squeeze her thighs together. She held out her hand. "Come to me, Leighton."

CHAPTER THIRTEEN

*S*helburn made a dog's dinner of taking off his breeches, largely because his attention was devoted to Kate's glorious body spread out across the tumbled sheets.

Her skin was perfect ivory, and her breasts swelled as the nipples beaded. He drew the scent of her arousal into his nostrils, edged with the cedar perfume of the soap that he'd used to wash her.

It had been so satisfying to serve her. Not just the pleasure of touching those long limbs and the smooth flesh. He was a few short hours into this love affair and already it took him way beyond his usual boundaries. Another boundary dissolved when he'd derived profound pleasure from ensuring her comfort. Sponging the traces of lovemaking from her body had roused an unfamiliar reverence.

Kate Starr was a dangerous woman. All the more dangerous because her unassuming air lured a man into a net of enchantment before he'd recognized his peril.

At last, he was naked, and he stepped toward the bed. But she slid forward until her elegant feet hit the floor. "You said I can touch you this time."

Oh, yes, please. Excitement jolted Shelburn so hard that his ears rang. He gulped for air and stopped a short space away.

Through the thunder in his eardrums, he watched her lift her hand. It came within an inch of his yearning cock, before her courage failed and she snatched it back.

His groan was long and heartfelt. If she meant to tease him, he wasn't sure that he'd survive the experience.

She sent him an uncertain glance. "What should I do?"

He caught her trembling hand and placed it on him. Her touch was cool on his fiery hot skin. The sensation blasted him like exploding gunpowder. "Curl your hand around me."

She bit her lip, as she fitted her hand to his erection with a firmness that startled him into a gasp.

"Should I stop?"

His grip calmed the fingers fluttering under his. "Don't you bloody dare."

He watched confidence seep into her expression. When she squeezed him with a tentative eagerness that threatened to pulverize him, he groaned again.

"More," he gritted out, as pleasure turned his blood molten.

"How..."

He was so het up that he was clumsy, trying to show her what he wanted. Kate caught on fast enough, nonetheless. Thank heaven for clever women.

His hand fell away from hers, as he realized that she was ready to follow her inclinations. When she closed her fist around him, he released a long, broken breath. He closed his eyes, as she shifted her hand up then down again.

"Yes," he hissed. "More."

She stroked him once more, before her thumb brushed the sensitive head. More heat. He tilted his hips forward to encourage her.

Her hand glided down to the nest of black curls at the base. "What do you call this?"

Opening glazed eyes, he struggled to make sense of her question. Difficult when he had trouble remembering his own name. "What you're doing?"

"No." As she stared at where she tormented him, her face was intent. That burning attention was almost as arousing as her touch. "Your...your male member. Is that what I should call it?"

One hand caught the back of her skull and held her in place for a fierce kiss. When he raised his head, he smiled down at her. "Men use a lot of names for their sexual organs. None of them are acceptable in polite society."

She squeezed him again, making his balls tighten with agony. One day, he'd pump his seed into her hand. One day, perhaps he'd even persuade her to take him into her mouth.

But not today. Today, he was too aware that he'd only been inside her once. He was desperate for more of that sizzling intimacy.

"I don't care about polite society." Her lips, red and full after his kisses, curved in a greedy smile. "But I want to know how to talk about this part of you that does such marvelous things to me."

"Kate, you're wonderful," he managed to force out of a throat as taut as the head of a drum.

Her unimpressed glance made him want to kiss her again. "I'm sure you'd say that to any woman who had her hand around your—"

Her daring startled him into an amused snort. "Cock."

"Is that what I should say?"

"It will serve. As I said, there are lots of names."

Her grip tightened, and she measured his length again. "Like what?"

"Prick. Dick." He sounded like he was strangling. "Penis. Staff. Mast. Peter."

Her nose wrinkled. "Peter?"

"Please don't use that."

"I won't."

"Pecker. Willie. John Thomas. Tackle. Captain. Third leg. Sword. Pickle." His lips twitched. "Mighty purple tree of power."

Her eyes rounded, as her thumb caressed the head of his penis. At this rate, he wasn't going to last. "No! That's just awful."

It hurt to laugh, but her horrified reaction was so priceless, he couldn't help it. "I might have made up that last one."

"But all the others are true?"

"Yes."

She stared down at his dick as if she pondered a mathematical equation, while her hand worked sin on his flesh. When that eager hand cupped his aching balls, his heart leaped up to lodge in his throat. He struggled not to spill.

"It's too big for a pickle."

Shelburn laughed again, which took him further along the road to losing control. He caught her hand and lifted it away. "Lie back, Kate. Now."

The last word emerged with an edge that he regretted, but between the dirty talk and her conscientious efforts to arouse him, he was in a fever to have her.

He wouldn't blame her if she cut up rough at receiving such a command. She wasn't the most docile of beings, and he had no illusions that she'd obey him just because men ordering women around was the accepted way of things.

But as Kate lifted her legs onto the bed and stretched out, her eyes were bright with excitement.

By God, he hoped that the last little while had excited her as much as it had excited him. He couldn't manage extended preliminaries. He dove down over her and even through his ravening hunger, he noted how she twined her arms around him and cradled him between her thighs.

When he found her sleek and primed, it wasn't a complete surprise. Even before he touched her sex, Shelburn had caught the earthy scent of her need.

"Don't wait," she said as he stroked her cleft.

Shelburn was past the point of holding back. He pushed forward, praying that he didn't hurt her again. But this time, her body flowered around him with immediate welcome. He was too stirred up for a long loving. From the first, he went deep.

She cried out in joy and lifted her hips to greet him. The agitated rhythm of her fingers kneading his shoulders spurred his drive to completion.

At the peak of each thrust, she tightened around him and sent stars shooting through his veins. The pleasure was so intense that he yearned to prolong it. But a storm of invincible hunger descended. He succumbed to an arduous release, just as Kate hurtled into her own climax.

When at last he returned to his surroundings, Kate's arms and legs trapped him against her in a glorious tangle. His face was buried in her hair, and his heaving chest crushed her breasts.

She still quaked with pleasure. Shelburn was damned grateful that she'd found her peak. That fast, wild ride hadn't done her justice.

Losing himself inside her had been a supreme moment. When she'd taken his seed, he'd...

Oh, hell. Hell. Hell. Hell.

How the devil had he let this happen? He couldn't believe that he'd forgotten his obligations to his partner so disastrously. What a complete dunderhead he was. He deserved a good horsewhipping.

"Kate?" he said, kissing her neck through the curtain of disordered hair.

"Mmm?" She stroked his back and despite everything, something in his soul expanded under the gentle caresses.

By God, he should be frantic about what just happened. If he'd made Kate pregnant, their lives would change forever.

He leaned on his elbows so he could see her face. Twilight revealed the rosy satisfaction that softened her features. The hazel gaze that rested on his face was more gold than green. Her eyes turned that color when she was happy.

By Jericho, she wouldn't be happy after he confessed his wrongs against her. He should pull out of her body. Another sign of the thrall she held him in – thrall to the point of arrant stupidity, damn it – that he couldn't yet bring himself to end their physical connection.

He stayed where he was. The harm had already been done, so he might as well bask in a physical well-being that made a nonsense of his howling conscience. Once again, he struggled to summon up a trace of genuine regret, but it remained absent.

God help him, climaxing inside Kate had been marvelous. The most marvelous moment that he could remember.

The ghost of that elation lingered. Despite his brain telling him that he was an irresponsible sod and that the consequences could be catastrophic.

Her rapt expression as she stared at him made him feel like a prince. By jingo, she wouldn't think that he was a prince, once he told her what had just happened. She might decide that she wanted nothing more to do with such a cad.

Which meant that before he spoke, he kissed her with weary thoroughness. Just in case he never got to kiss her again. She tasted weary, too. So it seemed absurd that as he lingered over her lips, desire should stir.

"This is what should happen afterward," she murmured, as he lifted his head.

"Yes." He flinched to recall his boorish behavior, following their first encounter. When the impact of what they'd just shared had stolen his capacity for speech.

Kate had a bad habit of sending him toppling over cliffs that he had no idea loomed ahead. He had a bad habit of forgetting that with Kate Starr, none of his previous experience counted to his advantage.

He kissed her again, then shifted to watch her face. "You're perfect. A daring partner. A woman who takes my breath away."

To his surprise, she looked nonplussed. "That's...lovely. Even if you don't mean it."

He frowned. "Devil take you, of course I mean it. I'm besotted, in case you haven't noticed."

Pure pleasure made her radiant. "Really?"

"Really. You must have guessed that you turn my world upside down. I don't know what special magic you possess, Kate, but it's damned powerful."

She lifted her head to kiss him. As always when she took the initiative, there was an extra dollop of sweetness that melted him into a bundle of longing.

"I'm putting a spell on you, Leighton Anstey. I claim you as my devoted slave for as long as we stay in this room."

Kate respected the bounds that he'd set for their affair. So why the deuce did her words strike him as so infernally unsatisfying?

Shelburn made himself smile, but it was an effort when it damn well shouldn't have been. "Your devoted slave is crushing you."

Most of his weight rested on his elbows, but he was a big man and he was sprawled across her. She must be uncomfortable, even if she did her best to get close enough to burrow inside him.

Guilt stabbed him, as he realized that he still had to deliver the bad news.

Regretting the separation the moment it occurred, he pulled free. So it seemed natural to sit up against the headboard and tug her into his side.

The connection returned, almost as nice as being inside her. Most of all when she shaped herself against him and his arm snaked behind her back to curl around until he cupped her breast.

He hadn't paid enough attention to those pretty breasts. Next time, he must remedy that.

The thought struck him that even now, her slender form might nurture his child. He waited for the sick feeling to descend. But the contentment that he'd found in taking Kate seemed to have chased away all his terror of leaving her with a bastard.

That made no sense. The true extent of their dilemma mustn't have struck him yet.

He squeezed her breast and struggled to ignore her voluptuous sigh of response. "Kate, did you notice something the last time we came together?"

She tugged the covers up to her waist and rested her head on his shoulder. "Well, I liked it. And you were in an almighty rush, which was very exciting."

"I'm glad you enjoyed it. So did I." She was either too innocent or too preoccupied with her burgeoning sensuality to pay attention. "Too much."

She stiffened in his hold and sat up straight. "I don't understand."

He sighed and brushed the heavy fall of hair away from her face. He loved her hair. "I didn't withdraw."

The words fell between them like rocks crashing down a mountainside. Kate slipped out of his hold. Yet again, he missed the connection the moment that it was broken.

When she didn't say anything straightaway, he rushed on. "I'm sorry. I don't blame you if you're furious. This has never happened to me before, and it shouldn't have happened now. Our love affair isn't progressing like my other love affairs do."

Those marked dark brows drew together, more in thoughtfulness than anger. That considered reaction was very like her. Kate, in contrast to most of his previous mistresses, wouldn't pitch china around the room and shriek to the rafters. "So you might have made me pregnant?"

He struggled to muster the requisite horror. He should be bloody horrified. Yet something stupid and possessive and primitive relished the thought of this magnificent creature carrying his child. He must be insane.

It was his turn to frown. "What will you do?"

Wide eyes, now more green than gold, met his searching gaze. "You don't owe me anything."

That wasn't the answer that he wanted, although God knew what answer he did want. It wasn't even the right answer, because if he'd got her with child, he most definitely owed her quite a lot.

But he was wise enough to reserve that argument for another day. After all, it was too soon to know whether his lack of control would bear fruit.

"This could destroy your life. Our association doesn't need to dog your footsteps forever. Hard to hide what you've been up to if in nine months, you produce an infant."

She continued to look thoughtful. "Do you hate the idea of me having your baby?"

Far from it. In fact, it was disturbing quite how much he did like it.

That was a first. He'd never had any great ambition to produce the next generation of Ansteys, although his duty to the title meant that he must marry sometime. His bride would likely be a girl with more hair than wit, one of the horde of blue-blooded misses who infested London's ballrooms every season.

He couldn't be less enthusiastic about the prospect.

"No, I don't hate it," he said. "But you should."

"Because of my good name?"

"Yes."

She tugged the sheet up to cover her breasts, which struck him as a pity. Even in the middle of a full-blown crisis, he couldn't ignore how desirable she was.

After a thorny silence, she spoke with characteristic composure. "I'm not an aristocratic lady guarding her chastity because the integrity of some noble line depends on it. Now that my engagement to Mr. Williams has fallen through, I have no plans to marry. Ever. I didn't even particularly want to marry him, but Alfred was so eager for the match and it made business sense. Not to mention it offered the chance to have children. Since I lost Sylvie and Mother and Da, I've missed being part of a loving family. Perhaps all this is fated. I may end up with a son or daughter to nurture. I'm sure Miss Donald will be willing to help me with a baby – and I'm on my way to see her once I leave you."

Leave him? What bloody nonsense was this? They'd only just begun. How dare she start planning the end of the affair already?

But more urgent than her departure was the issue of her possible pregnancy. Shocked, he stared at her. "You can't want to have a child out of wedlock."

"Can't I?" Her gaze remained steady. "It gives me a family without having to deal with a man's interference."

Shelburn bit back the objection that he'd very much want to interfere. Surely when he resumed his real life with its parade of selfish pleasures, he'd forget quite how paternal the idea of Kate Starr having his baby made him. "What about your reputation in business?"

To his growing disbelief, she shrugged. With every second, he could see that she warmed to the idea of becoming a mother. This was the most bizarre conversation that he'd ever had in his life.

"I'm rich enough to circumvent a scandal. There must be ways to have a child in secret, then adopt it as my own."

Her outrageous reaction shouldn't anger him. He should be bloody relieved that she wasn't making a fuss. But something about her practical, self-sufficient response irked him. He wasn't sure why, but her complete lack of interest in inviting his involvement in rearing their child felt like an insult.

"You've got it all planned out." Sourness edged his remark.

"It's too early to worry. In any case, I won't expect you to do the honorable thing."

That also sounded like an insult. As if neither of them could see him stepping up to take responsibility. "That's a relief to hear," he said with enough irony to make her frown again.

"I assumed you'd be glad to know that this isn't a complete disaster."

He shoved down the ridiculous hurt that her response sparked. Although she only said what she thought he wanted to hear, he'd had quite enough.

One thing emerged clear as crystal. From now on, he needn't pull out before his crisis. He could tumble Kate every which way from Sunday and finish inside her every time. Even in his current sulk, that sounded like bliss.

On the other hand, extending this pestilential conversation didn't sound at all like bliss. He'd enjoyed seducing Kate. More than enjoyed. But those charged moments when he'd pumped his seed into her had been the paramount experience of his debauched existence. He wanted more of that. He didn't want more of this damned unsettling discussion.

So he dragged her into his arms and began to kiss her as if he starved.

Looking delightfully flustered, she struggled out of his embrace. "Leighton! What are you doing?"

He placed one hand on her breast and rolled the nipple between his fingers until it was a hard point. "I'm furthering your education."

As he played with her breast, her eyes went glassy and her breath emerged in humid little gasps. "But we were talking about—"

"Later," Shelburn said with a hint of a snap, before he bent his head to suckle her other nipple.

To hell with it, he didn't want to talk. He didn't want to contemplate the future, with or without her. That way lay trouble, and he was in no mood for trouble. Instead, he wanted Kate thinking of nothing else but the sensual fire that raged between them.

CHAPTER FOURTEEN

Kate stirred to the sound of birdsong from the trees outside. Leighton lay behind her in the bed that had become her entire world over the last three days. He pressed up against her back, and his hand curved around her naked breast with a tender care that melted her heart.

To her chagrin, there had been far too many moments over the last days that had melted her heart.

She blinked eyes scratchy with too little sleep. And with tears that she refused to shed. She'd have plenty of time to cry, once she got back to Bradbourne. A whole lifetime.

She'd come to recognize that her situation was hopeless. She'd entered this affair in love with a fantasy. Three days of Lord Shelburn's constant company meant that she was now fathoms deep in love with the real man.

Kate had to leave while she still had the strength to go. She couldn't face another mortifying conversation, where his eyes turned to ice and he informed her that she was a fool to imagine anything stronger than ephemeral desire united them.

But, dear Lord in heaven, it was hard to go.

Which made it even more urgent that she went straightaway.

She wasn't sure of the time, but she guessed that it must be about five. As she'd succumbed to the sensual universe, time had lost all meaning.

Dawn light edged the drawn curtains and allowed her to make out the room's details. It was only about an hour since she and Leighton had crashed into an exhausted sleep after a furious interlude when she'd ridden him to a gasping climax. The scent of passion lingered in the air.

Trying not to wake her sleeping lover, she gently shifted his hand from her breast and slid toward the edge of the bed. She'd managed to sit up when to her alarm, he rolled onto his back and opened heavy eyes.

"Kate?"

She stood, praying her shaky knees would support her, and glanced back. She'd hoped to accomplish her ends without disturbing him. "Get some sleep, Leighton. It's been a long night."

His smile conveyed weariness and satisfaction. "Long and glorious."

It had been, even though she tried not to think about that. Their immediate physical compatibility had blossomed into hour after hour of sublime pleasure. Every time their bodies joined together, she thought that the experience couldn't get any better.

Then it did.

How in heaven's name was she going to survive without him?

With a heavy heart, she leaned down to kiss him, her hair slithering over one shoulder in an untidy tumble. His lips tasted of the brandy that they'd drunk in the middle of the night.

Although she knew that she just stored up heartache to come, she extended the kiss, imprinting every detail on her mind.

As she withdrew, Leighton caught her hand. "Come back to bed," he murmured in that raspy voice that made her very skin yearn.

"In a moment," she said, struggling to keep her tone light. She kissed him again, then wandered with manufactured nonchalance toward the door to the sitting room.

Over the last days, she'd become used to being naked in his presence. Now she felt him watch her from behind, and the knowledge that she'd never be naked with him again made her stomach cramp with longing.

"Don't be long," he said on a yawn.

"I won't be," she whispered as she left the room.

It was a lie, but a necessary one. With luck, Leighton would doze off and give her the chance to get away. She couldn't bear the idea of a scene. Not when it was likely to end with her humiliated and begging him to love her. When she knew he never would. Hadn't he told her so?

Kate threw on the clothes that she'd folded on the armchair beside the fire last night. Using the mirror over the fireplace, she did her best to fix her hair. Nobody would call her efforts a success, but they'd have to do.

Sneaking away like this marked her as a vile coward. Her harrowing emotions included a large dose of shame. It would be braver to face Leighton and tell him that it was time to part, and she'd always tried so hard to be brave.

But her plight eroded all courage. She feared that if he pleaded for her to stay, she'd give in, which only meant a more agonizing farewell to come. And she wasn't sure that her heart could survive, if he took the news of her departure in his stride.

After all, they'd both recognized from the first that this affair couldn't last more than a day or two. Apart from that prickly discussion about a possible pregnancy, they hadn't talked about the future at all.

Why would they? He'd made it clear that he had an itch to scratch, but that he intended to resume his dissolute life in London, once he'd worked off his interest in Kate.

Despite her urgency, she stopped at the door leading out to the corridor and looked around her. What had happened in these rooms had changed her forever. She'd never forget what she'd done here and how she'd felt, even when she was a lonely old woman.

Then recognizing that hesitation only put off the evil moment when she resumed her place as Kate Starr, canny mill owner and dedicated spinster, she eased the door open and slipped into the hallway.

Her reticule contained plenty of money, more than enough to hire a carriage and driver to take her away from the wicked Earl of Shelburn forever.

Shelburn collapsed back against the pillows and closed heavy eyes. By Jupiter, he was tired. His innocent mistress had introduced him to a whole new world of sensation, and the hours had passed in a blaze of passion. He was drifting off again, when he thought that he heard the faint snick of a door closing in the other room.

That was odd.

His sleep-fogged brain was slow to make sense of that sound. He burrowed deeper under the covers.

The morning was cold. Or perhaps he missed holding Kate, loose-limbed and luscious in his arms. He adored using her long, vigorous body. But he also adored snuggling up beside her, breathing in the scent of well-satisfied woman and feeling her cling to him as she sought sleep. Not that either of them had slept much since they'd come to the inn.

He'd never known days like these last three. He'd never known a lover like Kate.

So where in Hades was she? He'd assumed that she'd sought privacy in the dressing room, but it was easier to go through from the bedroom. And she'd been away a long time, if her purpose was to seek the chamber pot.

The mists of weariness evaporated, as a completely unacceptable premonition descended.

He bolted upright against the pillows, alert to the sounds of someone moving about outside the bedroom. But the apartment was silent. Something grim in his soul told him that the silence came from absence.

What the devil?

His heart started racing as if he'd run up a mountain, and his blood froze. He rolled out of bed and rushed naked out into the parlor.

No Kate.

Knowing that he wasted his time, he checked the dressing room. Empty.

Sucking in a deep breath to calm his rising panic, he went through the apartment with more care. Her clothes were gone. He stopped in the center of the parlor, in the place where he'd first kissed her, and struggled to accept that she'd gone.

Every cell of his body rose in shrieking denial. Why would she go when they'd been so happy? Surely she'd tell him if she'd decided to end things. He'd always admired her candor.

Kate wasn't the sort of woman to scuttle away, as if what they'd done was a dirty secret. One of the many things he liked about her was her lack of shame about becoming his lover.

Was he overreacting?

Perhaps she'd gone downstairs for something. But what? It was so early, and neither of them had sought sustenance outside these rooms since they'd arrived.

Had she decided to write to her cousins – who sounded like a rum pair in his opinion – to say that she was safe? Leighton was more than happy to let the world wend on its merry way while he remained lost to pleasure, but Kate was more conscientious than that.

The logical part of his mind knew that he clutched at straws. There was no reason for anyone to send a message at this absurd hour. But he resisted accepting that she'd taken off without a word. After all the radiant intimacy that they'd shared, she couldn't be so cruel.

He was worried and increasingly angry. But most of all, he was hurt – which was a new experience for the heartless Earl of Shelburn. While he might desire a woman, his love affairs never engaged his deeper emotions.

But over these last days, he'd come to trust Kate, and he thought that she'd come to trust him. Flitting away in the dawn light without warning or explanation was a betrayal of that trust.

So Shelburn flung on his breeches and shirt and boots and ventured outside. As he descended the staircase for the first time in three days, the inn was quiet around him.

Once he reached the ground floor, he started searching for a servant. Hearing clattering from the kitchens, he turned down another flagstoned corridor.

He passed empty taprooms and private parlors. During the preceding centuries, the rambling building had been added to over and over, so it was a maze of winding corridors and different levels. No sign of Kate anywhere.

The unwelcome idea that she'd indeed left him grew more clamorous, but he refused to give up hope. He'd never felt such closeness to a lover. She wouldn't leave him flat.

When he met a maid scrubbing a narrow hallway, she lurched to her feet and curtsied.

"My...my lord," the girl stammered. Her wide-eyed regard told him that he wasn't at his sartorial best. Which was something the elegant Earl of Shelburn never said. While his morals might verge on the mucky, he was always dressed *comme il faut*.

"I'm looking for Miss Starr." He resisted the urge to tuck in the shirt flapping loose around his hips and to tidy his hair. Before he came downstairs, he hadn't even combed it. He also desperately needed a shave.

Although he struggled not to glower like an angry lion, he doubted that he succeeded, because the girl looked more nervous by the second. She spoke in a breathless hurry. "The lady left in a hired carriage, my lord. Will, the junior groom, is driving her."

She'd gone.

Shelburn felt like some great bruiser of a prizefighter had slugged him in the guts. All the air rushed out of his lungs, and the world went cold and dark. He couldn't pretend anymore that he'd mistaken what her absence meant. She'd abandoned him to return to her real life, a real life that held no place for her disreputable lover.

He came back to himself to see the girl holding out a sealed paper. "She left this for you, sir."

Shelburn grabbed it with a rudeness that he couldn't help. Perhaps this would explain Kate's departure. Even better, include a promise to come back.

He became aware of the maid's unhidden curiosity. He retained enough *amour propre* to wait until he was alone to open Kate's letter. "Thank you," he bit out.

"Very good, sir."

The girl curtsied again, as he marched away at a speed that he feared betrayed his agitation. The moment that he turned into an empty corridor, he stopped and ripped the letter open with shaking hands. Kate must have had some good reason for this sudden departure.

Reading the note took him two seconds. He crushed the paper into a tight ball, which he tossed into the first fireplace he found.

Then he returned to the foyer and mounted the stairs two at a time to the rooms where for such an excruciatingly short period, he'd dwelled in paradise.

Be damned to Kate Starr. How dare she leave him with such discourtesy? Plague take her, he deserved better.

His pride smarted under the insult. He'd show that impertinent vixen that nobody trifled with the feelings of Leighton Anstey, Earl of Shelburn.

CHAPTER FIFTEEN

Any hopes of finding a refuge with her old governess, where she could nurse her earth-shattering sorrow, dissolved the moment that Will pulled the gig up outside Miss Donald's whitewashed cottage in Heddle End.

Kate surveyed the expensive conveyance parked on the grass verge outside the privet hedge dividing Miss Donald's garden from the road. Her heart, already tried to the point of splitting, sank into her expensive half boots.

She knew that carriage. It had carried Jebediah Williams to Bradbourne, where he'd made his unemotional proposal to merge businesses and lives. Kate had dearly hoped that she might escape another face-to-face encounter with Mr. Williams. It seemed that she'd hoped in vain. More cowardice, she admitted, but she'd planned to break her engagement with a letter.

Right now, the idea of having to explain herself to a jilted suitor made her feel sick. She placed one hand over her heaving stomach and contemplated asking Will to drive her on to Stevenage, where she could arrange transport back home.

Although she supposed that if Mr. Williams had taken the trouble to track her down in Hertfordshire, he wouldn't hesitate to follow her to Derbyshire to get an explanation for her rash behavior.

"This be the place you want, miss?" Will asked, as his passenger remained unmoving in the seat beside him.

"Yes, it is." She'd visited Miss Donald several times in the last ten years, so she knew her way around the village.

Kate squared her shoulders and told herself that if she could take over Starr Cotton Mills as a grief-stricken girl of twenty, she could handle a disappointed wooer. Except that right now, she was struggling to come to terms with losing the only man she'd ever loved. Fate could have given her a chance to lick her wounds, before flinging her back into the hurly-burly.

Fate, it turned out, was a spiteful shrew.

"Miss Starr?" Will asked again as the silence persisted. "Shall I help you down?"

She clenched her gloved hands and told herself that she would *not* cry. It would be the absolute last straw to turn up at her old governess's door, looking like she was ashamed of what she'd done. It was bad enough that she arrived with her hair a mess, crumpled clothes, and Leighton's scent on her skin. "No, thank you. I can manage."

I can manage.

Someone would put those words on her tombstone, she feared. And the truth was that she could manage. But nobody ever seemed to ask what it cost her to manage. Right now, she wondered why she bothered.

Chin up, Kate. You're frightening the help.

She climbed out of the gig and even found it in her to smile at Will and thank him and send him on his way back to the Merry Haymaker with a substantial tip.

She stepped forward on wobbly legs and unlatched the picket gate leading into Miss Donald's neat front garden, bright with spring flowers. The display of colorful garden beds only mocked Kate's misery. The world around her rushed toward summer, whereas she felt like she'd dwell in freezing winter for the rest of her life.

When the green wooden door ahead opened to reveal Hazel, Kate wasn't surprised. How else had Mr. Williams tracked her to this obscure village? Her cousin must have told him about Miss Donald.

"Kate!" Hazel said in such exaggerated horror that, despite everything, she almost laughed. One would think a murderer marched up the path with blood dripping from his hands, instead of one very chastened woman. A woman who needed to make her peace with the barren desert of a life extending before her.

"Good morning, Hazel," she said calmly.

"Good morning? *Good morning?* When we feared you were dead? When you drove off with a man notorious the country over for ruining woman after woman? When it's been three days without a peep from you?" Hazel was back to flapping her hands in front of her face. "We waited in London, sure you'd see sense, but when you didn't show up, we went to Hatfield. But they had no knowledge of you there. We've been to half the towns in Hertfordshire, trying to find you. Thank goodness, I remembered your old governess. You've put us all to so much trouble and worry. Yet you have the gall to turn up, and all you have to say for yourself is good morning? Kate Starr, you should hang your head in shame. You should blush and beg our forgiveness. You should—"

Kate raised a hand to stem the flow of hysterical chastisement. "I think you should stop before you say something I won't forgive."

It was a barely veiled threat. While her cousins had been helpful up until now, they weren't quite as necessary to Kate as they imagined they were.

Hazel's eyes bulged, and she gasped at Kate's effrontery. She staggered back to collide with her husband, who loomed up behind her. With little ceremony, he pushed her aside. Alfred and Hazel's marriage lacked tenderness, Kate had long ago noticed.

"So you decided to show up at last, did you?" The sneering question made Kate itch to punch his nose. Most of the time, she could handle Alfred and Hazel. But this morning, she was far from her usual competent self.

"Good morning, Alfred," she said coldly, refusing to defend herself for running off with Leighton. She owed this man nothing. In fact, he should be grateful that she gave him a good wage and a luxurious home, not that he ever acknowledged his obligation.

It offended him to see a female in authority over men. He'd always considered himself a more appropriate person to run the mills, even though in business terms, Kate had never put a foot wrong and when he'd moved into her house, she'd had to rescue him from the verge of bankruptcy.

To her relief, Miss Donald called from inside. "For heaven's sake, let the girl come in off the doorstep before you give her a tongue-lashing. The neighbors have had more than enough entertainment today."

Kate was sure that they had. She'd already noticed curtains twitching in the cottage next door.

With reluctance, Alfred moved aside, and his grip on a drooping Hazel looked no more enthusiastic. Miss Donald appeared in the hallway behind them.

For the first time since she'd left Walford, a genuine smile curled Kate's lips. Hilda Donald had taught the two Starr sisters with affection and good sense. The prospect of sinking into her governess's embrace brought tears to her eyes. While Miss Donald might think that her former charge had been a fool, she'd love her all the same.

"Donny, I must beg your pardon. I seem to have brought chaos down on you."

Her governess smiled, as if nothing pleased her more on a fine Wednesday morning than an errant ex-student turning up at her door. "They haven't been here very long. And it's always a treat to see you, Kate, whatever the circumstances. Come in and have tea."

When Donny held her hands out, Kate took them gratefully. The unconditional welcome made her aching heart cramp. She blinked away more tears.

Damn Leighton. He turned her into a watering pot.

"Thank you," she whispered, as she surged forward for a hug.

"There's another one in the parlor," Miss Donald murmured in her ear.

Of course there was. Kate still had to deal with her former fiancé. "I'll get rid of them, then I'll tell you everything."

Well, perhaps not *everything*.

"I gather you've been busy having adventures."

Alfred was close enough to hear that, and he puffed up in outrage. "You cannot mean to abet this woman's corruption. Three days ago, she disappeared in the company of a known seducer, and nobody's heard a word from her since. One doesn't need to try too hard to imagine the depravity she's been up to."

"Mr. Mercer, this is my house. I say who is welcome here and who isn't." Miss Donald regarded Alfred with a weary dislike that had developed remarkably fast, Kate noted. "At least most of the time."

Alfred ignored the barbed comment. The door at the end of the corridor opened. Kate's stomach dipped again, as Jebediah Williams appeared. He was tall and distinguished, and his manner was smooth, but there was a chill in his gray eyes that she'd never liked.

Thank you, Leighton. Whatever happens after this, at least I'll never marry this self-satisfied prig.

It wasn't much consolation, when she'd mourned the loss of her wild lover from the moment that she'd forsaken him. Nothing Alfred or Hazel – or Mr. Williams – could say, however hurtful, could compete with the agony of knowing that she'd never see Leighton again.

"Miss Starr, can you spare me a few minutes?" Mr. Williams's voice was cold. But then, his voice was always cold.

Kate braced herself, while Miss Donald turned on him. "The poor lamb has just arrived. At least let her wash her hands and have a morsel to eat before you start haranguing her."

Mr. Williams looked offended. "I have no intention of haranguing her, my good woman. But as we are to be married, I believe Miss Starr owes me an immediate account of her recent activities. That doesn't seem too much to ask. My concern for her insists upon it."

He didn't sound concerned. He sounded angry. Kate couldn't blame him, she supposed. She'd made promises to him, however half-hearted.

"Miss Donald, I'm prepared to speak to Mr. Williams." With a show of calm, she took off her gloves, her bonnet, and her pelisse. "The sooner we sort out this mess, the better."

"A mess isn't exactly how I'd describe your profligate behavior," Alfred snapped. "I'm ashamed to claim you as kin."

Kate had been referring to the strangers invading her governess's small cottage, but she bit her lip to contain her sharp response. "Mr. Williams, I'm at your disposal. Perhaps we could retire to the parlor for a little privacy? Miss Donald, is that acceptable to you?"

Her governess took the outdoor clothing from Kate. "I don't like to think of him bullying you."

"I don't let anyone bully me," Kate said with a staunchness that she didn't feel. Especially as it was now much too clear that she'd let Alfred bully her into accepting this engagement.

"I will treat Miss Starr with all consideration," Mr. Williams said.

Kate was far from sure of that, but this would be the last time that she'd have to deal with him. She could be strong for just a little longer.

Then Mr. Williams would leave, and she'd send Alfred and Hazel on their way, too. She could indulge in the luxury of a good cry and a sympathetic ear that belonged to someone who really did have her best interests at heart. Miss Donald's kindness wouldn't heal her wounded soul, but it might stop her feeling like she'd swallowed broken glass.

"Mr. Williams, shall we conclude our business?" she asked with the coolness that she'd learned to feign over all these years.

He stood back, as she walked along the short hall and entered the parlor. When he closed the door, she tried to conceal her nerves. She owed this man an apology. Better that it was an apology Alfred couldn't interrupt with sanctimonious pronouncements.

Mr. Williams remained near the door while Kate stood in the middle of the room. He folded his arms and regarded her as if she was a naughty schoolgirl. "What do you have to say for yourself, Miss Starr?"

"I have no regrets about my actions." She didn't like his superior manner, but she had wronged him, so with difficulty, she maintained a pleasant tone. "However, I don't blame you for feeling ill-used. I gave you to understand that I'd marry you."

When he tried to interrupt, she raised her chin and went on. "I accept that our engagement is at an end. You're free to walk away, secure in the knowledge that we would never have suited. Let's give thanks that the match won't proceed. It promised neither of us happiness."

Instead of the relief that she expected to see, Mr. Williams was frowning. "You mistake me, Miss Starr. I insist that our engagement stands."

She regarded him with astonishment and confusion. Her former betrothed should be on his knees, thanking his Creator for saving him from such an unsuitable match. Jebediah Williams placed great store in respectability, she knew.

Perhaps he misunderstood what she was trying to tell him, although he must know that she'd become Leighton's lover. Alfred had no doubts about what she'd been doing.

For pity's sake, Mr. Williams just needed to look at her. She'd done her best to present a tidy appearance when she left the Merry Haymaker, but she was queasily aware that she looked like she'd just crawled out of a man's bed.

Her voice hardened. "I just spent three days alone with a man to whom I'm not married. You have every right to be furious."

"I'm not furious." He sounded like he was furious. Or at least that he was doing his inadequate best to hide it.

"No man wants his future wife entangled with a philanderer."

"No, he doesn't. But your indiscretions don't necessarily make you an unacceptable wife."

None of this made any sense. "Yes, they do."

He ignored her. "I doubt there will be a scandal. According to Mr. Mercer, nobody recognized you at the Angel. Even if Lord Shelburn bandies your name about, the gossip won't penetrate our less rarefied circles. I do believe, though, that it's best for all concerned if you retire from running the mills after the wedding."

Kate resented the suggestion that she should shroud herself away like a dirty secret. "Don't you care that I betrayed you?"

"Ours is not a union based on foolish emotion, but on sound business principles. Those principles haven't changed."

She straightened and sent him a direct look. She refused to believe that his masculine pride – Mr. Williams was a stiff-necked, proud man – could stomach a wife of less than stellar chastity. Nor did his calmness convince her "But I've changed, Mr. Williams. I no longer wish to marry you."

This time, Kate caught the flare of rage in his eyes before he masked it. She realized that it had never occurred to him that even if he was willing to overlook her behavior, she might reject him. He expected her to fling herself on his mercy and beg his forgiveness. No wonder he looked as if he'd swallowed a lemon.

His prominent jaw set in a mulish line. "I won't release you from this engagement."

"I'm afraid you must, because I won't marry you."

He looked more sour by the second. "That's not an acceptable answer."

"I'm sorry you feel that way. There's—"

"I could sue you for breach of promise."

She'd never much liked Mr. Williams. Now she began to actively despise him. What on earth had possessed her to agree to marry him? "You could, but that won't gain my cooperation and it will create a scandal where, as you pointed out, at present there is none."

"You won't like your name dragged through the mud, Miss Starr."

"I won't. But pardon my frankness, I'd like being your wife even less."

When he lurched toward her, she struggled not to flinch back. To her relief, he sucked in a deep breath and the threat of violence receded. "I would ask you to do me the courtesy of reconsidering. You should be grateful that I'm willing to stand by you in your disgrace."

"I'm sure I—"

He spoke over her. He hadn't in their earlier meetings, but she had a premonition that if, God forbid, she married him, she'd never again finish a sentence. "How long do you intend to stay in Heddle End?"

"A few days."

"In that case, I will call on you in Bradbourne next week and hope that you've come to your senses."

"There's no point. I won't—"

He bowed with a complete lack of deference and turned to go. "Your servant, Miss Starr."

CHAPTER SIXTEEN

*S*haking, Kate collapsed onto a chair in front of the unlit hearth. She told herself that she would not cry, she would not cry.

That interview with Mr. Williams had been awful. She'd prepared for him to rant and declare that he wanted nothing more to do with such a trollop. Learning that he sought to hold her to their betrothal left her upset and perplexed.

What self-respecting man would accept a woman who had just come from another fellow's bed? Perhaps if Mr. Williams loved her, she could understand it. But there had never been more than commerce and convenience between them.

"I brought you a cup of tea," Miss Donald said from the doorway. The hall behind her was empty. Her cousins and Mr. Williams must have gone out into the front garden. "I thought you might need it."

Kate looked up and struggled to smile, but she couldn't quite manage it. "Oh, Donny, what an awful mess I've got myself into."

Miss Donald stepped forward and slid the cup and saucer onto the table at Kate's elbow. "We'll sort things out, love."

While she appreciated her governess's optimism, Kate wasn't so sure. Leaving Leighton had carved a chasm in her heart that would never knit together. "First of all, we need to get rid of Mr. Williams and my cousins. I'm so sorry that you've been overrun."

Familiar amusement lit Donny's eyes. "Oh, it's a bit of excitement in a quiet life."

"You're so kind." This time, Kate did smile. "I shouldn't have come here. Although even if I hadn't, you'd still have to deal with all these people. You must be wishing me to Jericho."

"Not at all. You and Sylvie were the daughters I never had. Once we send these overbearing, useless men away, we'll sit down and have a good talk." Miss Donald had never held a high opinion of the male sex. As a lifelong devotee of Mary Wollstonecraft's philosophy, she'd instilled radical ideas of female independence into her students. "Everything can be fixed one way or another."

Donny was right. All was not lost. Kate needed to stop acting like a wet hen. She would survive this. She might emerge with a bruised and battered heart, but nonetheless she would emerge. She straightened from her despairing slump and picked up her tea.

She'd known when she went to Leighton's bed that her stay there would be brief. Alfred and Hazel might be outraged at this moment, but both enjoyed a comfortable life, thanks to her. They knew which side their bread was buttered on. Mr. Williams would accept his dismissal in the end, even if he didn't go as readily as she'd like. He couldn't drag her kicking and screaming to the altar and force her to speak her vows.

"I'm so glad I came, Donny." Kate took a restorative sip of tea.

"I'm glad you came, too. I know you write every week, but it's even better to have you here in my house."

"I've missed you."

"Stay as long as you like." Her old governess paused. "In fact, it's such a nice day, why don't you go out into the back garden and sit in the quiet for a while? I'll move these pests on without you worrying yourself. They won't gain the advantage over Hilda Donald."

They wouldn't. Donny might have always been kind and loving, but she hadn't put up with any nonsense either.

Carrying her cup and saucer, Kate rose as Donny crossed to open the French doors leading outside. "I can't thank you enough. I couldn't bear another scolding right now."

"You take your time, and once we've got the place to ourselves, you can tell me about the scrape you're in."

Kate's snort of amusement held a hint of tears. "You'll be appalled."

"I doubt it." Donny didn't smile. "I've lived on this earth for seventy years. It hasn't all been tea and chocolate eclairs."

Kate smiled at that and the smile lingered when she descended the steps. She settled in a patch of sun beneath one of the windows ranging on either side of the French doors. She appreciated a few moments on her own, when nobody was watching and she didn't have to hide her broken heart.

At least she now knew what love was. It was nothing like her mawkish imaginings when she retired alone to her bed after a long day at the mill. Love was physical and invincible and all-encompassing, a devotion that deepened with every heartbeat. While she'd been an impulsive fool and the consequences of her recklessness would cast a long shadow, she now had something glorious to remember. Right now, that didn't lessen her sorrow. But perhaps one day, it would.

She'd drifted into a miserable haze, almost a doze, when she heard voices from the parlor behind her. It seemed that Donny hadn't yet managed to dislodge either Alfred or Mr. Williams, although Kate couldn't imagine why they lingered.

"I'm not pleased with you, Mercer. I'm still shocked that you allowed this to happen." It was Mr. Williams, and now he made no attempt to hide his anger. "You said you had everything under control, yet it seems all our plans are in the balance."

"I'm sorry, sir. At the Angel, the brainless wench took off before we could stop her."

Brainless wench? Despite everything, Kate was surprised to hear Alfred speak of her with such contempt.

She pressed against the whitewashed wall at her back. Unless Alfred or Mr. Williams stood in front of the window and looked down, she was invisible from the house. She should tell them that she was listening, she supposed, but right now, the prospect of confronting either of them made her stomach roil with nausea.

"I hadn't thought she was so wild," Mr. Williams said.

"Neither did I." Alfred moved closer to the window. "But she'll come back into line. Does our arrangement stand?"

Arrangement? The word smacked of a conspiracy. A chill trickled down Kate's spine as she shrank into the wall. Any urge to announce her presence vanished.

"Why shouldn't it? I told you I'm a man of my word. You'll run the factories under my ownership, once your cousin and I are wed."

"You think she'll still have you?"

"Of course." The oily certainty in Mr. Williams voice made Kate feel bilious. "Right now, she's half-mad with lust, poor bitch, but once the reality of being ruined sinks in, she'll beg me to take her on."

"She can be stubborn."

"So can I." Mr. Williams paused. "In fact, her recent stupidity might play into our hands. Persuading the courts that my poor fragile wife is in no position to manage her affairs should prove no difficulty, once we report that she ran off with an acknowledged rake."

Alfred's laugh had Kate's trembling hands clenching in her skirts. After all she'd done for him, the slimy, lying swine had concocted this plot against her.

"You're right. And we have several hundred witnesses to her mania. Putting her away as a lunatic and taking control of the mills should be simple. She's stuck her own head into the noose. We just need to tighten the loop and all our hopes come to fruition." Alfred moved away from the window. "I'll try and talk her into coming to Bradbourne with us, but even if she stays here a few days, she'll want to get back to the mills. We'll see you in a week or so."

"That sounds like a plan."

Dumbfounded with horror and disbelief, Kate heard the door to the parlor open and shut. The villainy of what she'd just learned stretched beyond what she could credit. No wonder Williams persisted in his wish to marry her. He and her toad of a cousin had hatched this scheme to steal her inheritance and have her locked away in an asylum.

On wobbly legs, she rose and turned toward the doors. Thank heaven that she'd run off with Leighton before Williams put his plot into action. To think, she'd been on the verge of signing the marriage settlement, which contained that seemingly harmless clause about her husband taking control of her assets if she became incapacitated.

Harmless? Like hell. That had been the whole purpose of this devil's courtship. And her cousin's husband had abetted him all the way.

She still had difficulty accepting it. How did Alfred sit at her table every night, eating her food, accepting the wage she paid him, yet intend her such harm?

Did Hazel know about this plan? She must, Kate suspected.

This treachery bit deep. Hazel was the last of her family. Her cousins' attempt to defraud Kate of all that was rightfully hers left a sour taste in her mouth.

Temper rising, Kate squared her shoulders. These swindlers weren't going to get the better of her. Joseph Starr's daughter was too wily to fall for their tricks.

She marched through the empty parlor to find Donny, her cousins, and that snake Jebediah Williams gathered in the hall. Behind them, the front door was open onto the small front garden. The significance of where Kate appeared from made Alfred's eyes widen in alarm.

Well it should.

Hazel stepped toward her with a sympathetic smile that Kate no longer trusted. "Come home with us, dear. It's been an upsetting few days, and you need family around you at such a time."

Kate put aside the heartbroken lover and spoke like the woman who had run Starr Mills for ten years. "That's the last thing I need."

The flicker of dismay and guilt in her cousin's eyes was enough to confirm that Hazel knew about the plot to take control of the mills, even if she hadn't been an active participant.

"Kate?" Donny's concerned tone told Kate that despite her best efforts, she must look devastated.

She'd weep once her battle was done – and heaven knew, she had plenty to weep about. Right now, she needed to be as immovable as the granite tors on the moors that she walked over near Bradbourne.

Her voice emerged hard and cold as ice. "Mr. Williams, there will be no marriage, which means you'll have no chance to get your filthy paws on my factories."

He went white with rage, rage that she knew he'd been doing his best to hide. "Now, look here—"

Kate shook her head. "All dealings between us are over."

"Kate, what on earth has happened?" Hazel came up to take Kate's arm. "You're not yourself."

Kate shook Hazel off like the cockroach she was. "Don't pretend you weren't in on the scheme."

"What scheme?" Donny asked, looking puzzled.

"Mr. Williams and my loving family..." She bit out the last words with enough contempt to make Hazel flinch back. "...set up a plan to have me declared unfit to run my own affairs. Alfred was to take over the mills under Mr. Williams's ownership, while I languished in isolation as a supposed madwoman."

Donny gasped in shock. "That's heinous."

"Isn't it just?"

Alfred glared at her without a scrap of shame. "You're not fit to run the business. It's monstrous for a man to take orders from a flibbertigibbet with grand ideas. This latest escapade just proves my point."

Kate's lips tightened, as anger threatened to master her. "This latest escapade saved me from the biggest mistake of my life. No wonder you were so in favor of this match."

"You would have been well treated," Williams said. "We're not monsters."

Kate almost laughed at that. "No. You're thieves and liars and conspirators."

"Get out of my house," Donny said, sounding every inch the governess. "You are no longer welcome here."

Kate drew herself up to her considerable height. "Alfred and Hazel, I want you gone from my home, too. Pack up your belongings the minute you reach Bradbourne and get out of my sight."

Hazel went pale and staggered back. Perhaps at last she might indeed faint. "You can't—"

"I can."

"But we have nowhere to go."

"Perhaps Mr. Williams will take you in," Kate said with a poisonous sweetness that set her cousin sniveling.

Hazel fumbled in her pocket to find a handkerchief. "Kate, you can't be so cruel."

"Yes, I can," she said in a flinty voice. "And if I find anything missing from the house when I get back, I'll prosecute you for theft. Whatever the scandal. You've been living on my charity long enough, when this is the thanks I get for it."

"Alfred, tell her she's being unreasonable," Hazel wailed, sagging against the wall in the beginnings of a swoon.

"Shut up, Hazel," Alfred said without glancing at his wife.

His attention remained on Kate. He'd never done much to hide his dislike, but even so, the utter disgust in his expression shocked her. How on earth could she have lived with these two people without guessing the depth of their malice against her?

"I've worked for you for ten years," Alfred said in a strident voice. "The mills won't survive without me."

Alfred had always cherished an inflated opinion of his importance. "We'll see."

He surged forward and caught her arm. "I won't stand for this. You owe me more."

Williams loomed closer, too, and all of a sudden, Kate felt hedged in. Despite the fear freezing her blood, she glared at the two men. "There's no point threatening me."

"I'm taking you back to Bradbourne." Alfred's grip tightened to bruising. "You'll marry Mr. Williams, and you'll sign the mills over to him in the settlement. Or at least you will, if you know what's good for you."

"Let her go," Donny snapped. "I won't have a kidnapping from my front hall."

Staring into Alfred's eyes, Kate saw that his temper had taken control. She tried to wrench free, but to no avail.

"Let me go this instant, Alfred, or I'll have you up on a charge of assault." It became more and more difficult to maintain the imperious tone.

"What the devil are you doing, manhandling the woman I intend to marry?"

The crisp aristocratic baritone sliced through the rising hysteria like a knife through butter.

A shocked silence crashed down. Dazed, Kate peered past Alfred to see Leighton poised on the threshold, surveying the unruly crowd in the hallway with lordly displeasure.

CHAPTER SEVENTEEN

*S*helburn observed the brouhaha in front of him with a scowl, as he tried to make sense of what was happening. He remembered the drab middle-aged man and woman from London as Kate's cousins. The tall cove with graying hair and the hatchet face was a stranger, as was the older lady. Although an acquaintance with the breed told him that she must be Kate's former governess and the owner of the cottage.

Last of all, because most important, his attention leveled on Kate.

Since waking up without her this morning, the world had been out of tune and packed with thorns and pitfalls. Whatever spell she'd laid upon him, it was damned potent sorcery. Just the sight of her austere goddess's face was enough to calm his turmoil.

While seeing her might fill the gap that had opened inside him after her departure, it didn't soothe his hurt feelings. In general, he didn't indulge in the more emphatic emotions, but the last few days had changed that.

Right now, for example, he'd dearly love to run a sword through the odious fellow who put his hands on Kate. Nor did Shelburn miss the fear sparking in Kate's fine eyes.

By Jupiter, he'd also like to skewer the tall bugger who he assumed was the fiancé Williams.

What a sodding pity that he'd arrived unarmed, although his fists clenched at his sides in preparation for a fight. He'd have to rely on sheer bloody aristocratic arrogance to win the day.

He had more than enough of that.

"Leighton..." Kate stammered, and he drew an instant's pleasure from the flaring joy that transformed her face when she saw him.

He wasn't a man given to self-doubt, but on the drive to Heddle End, he'd found himself wondering if Kate had deserted him because she was no longer interested in staying. Her expression proved that whatever her reasons for going, distaste for her lover wasn't among them.

Thank the Lord.

Which raised the question of why the deuce she'd run off.

Shelburn intended to sort all that out, once he'd sent these inconvenient nobodies to Hades.

"Let Miss Starr go." He hardened his tone to the one that had the servants at Capstone Abbey jumping to obey. "Now."

As he'd expected, the voice of authority had immediate effect, and Kate was free. She rushed forward and extended shaking hands in his direction. "Take me away."

Shelburn seized her hands. The contact of skin on skin settled something troubled and unhappy within him. And made him all the hungrier to have her to himself again.

"If you like. After all, I live to serve you." It might sound like meaningless flattery, but it was nothing less than the truth. "Did he hurt you?"

"Kate, you can't go off with this man," the frump twittered behind her. "Have a thought for your reputation."

Without sparing the woman a glance, Kate shook her head. "No. You arrived in time. Lucky for me."

His jaw firmed. "Lucky for him, too."

"Don't...don't create a scandal here." Kate's fingers twined in his. "They're not worth it. I just want to go."

"My carriage is outside and at your disposal." Whatever drama he'd interrupted, some instinct told him that it was unimportant in the larger picture. What was important was keeping this outstanding woman by his side. Damn it, she never should have strayed in the first place.

Kate turned to meet the older lady's wise gray eyes. Some message passed between them, as she said, "Donny, shall we stay and see off this rabble?"

"Rabble?" Williams said on a rising intonation.

"If I can handle the Starr sisters, I can handle these three troublemakers."

"You don't mean to encourage this criminal recklessness?" the other man spluttered in horror.

"You're the criminal here," the lady said, her manner uncompromising.

As her cousin floundered under the accusation, Kate addressed him in a hard voice. "I'd avoid lingering too long in Hertfordshire, Alfred. The first chance I get, I mean to send a message to Bradbourne to change all the locks on the house and to forbid you permission to set foot on the mill premises. If you're not there before that to pack up your belongings, I'll give them to the poor."

"Kate, you've become so callous," the other woman sniffled.

She ignored the interruption with a haughty disdain that made Shelburn want to cheer. "Time is of the essence, and your return journey mightn't be straightforward. I suspect that you'll have to go all the way back to London to find a public coach service to Derbyshire. That is unless Mr. Williams intends to take you in his carriage. Although I wouldn't trust too much in his generosity, now that his plot has been thwarted."

"Let's go, Hazel." The man vibrated with offense. "I won't stay here and be insulted."

"Mr. Williams, you should go, too," Kate said, dislike dripping from her tone in a way that Shelburn could only commend.

He performed a cold bow. "Miss Starr, I begin to think that not even your riches could make me marry you."

Kate wasn't listening. Instead, she stood beside Shelburn and smiled up at him. "I'm so glad you came to find me."

He couldn't help smiling back, even if he was yet to learn why she'd left in the first place. It seemed an addlepated thing to do, when it was so blindingly obvious that they should be together. A bright woman like Kate Starr must see that, if a dunderhead like him could. "It looks like I arrived in the nick of time."

"Oh, we would have bested these ruffians," the older lady said, stepping forward to usher the three interlopers out of the door. "Although it was marvelous to see you swoop in to rescue my darling Kate. It quite made my staid old heart skip a beat, my lord."

The two men and the woebegone goose of a woman now huddled on the doorstep. Shelburn admired the sharp finality with which Miss Donald slammed the door after them and slid the bolt across.

Shelburn curled his arm around Kate, glorying in how she fitted herself into his side. His Minerva was the perfect height to match him. His Minerva was perfect for him in every way.

Miss Donald turned to Kate. "My dear, while I appreciate the romance of this scene, I'm not sure that it's proper for you to drive away alone with his lordship."

It wasn't. But then, their behavior hadn't been proper from the first. Kate blushed fiery red and looked charmingly young. Shelburn wished that he remembered meeting her all those years ago. She claimed that she'd been below his notice back then, but he didn't believe it.

"Donny, if you've picked up anything from today's melee, it must be that I'm already ruined." To his regret, Kate stepped away as she confessed her sins.

The older lady clicked her tongue in dismissal. "For shame, Kate, you should know that I judge a lady on more than her compliance with society's rules. I have no doubt that you've been a little reckless, but saying that you're ruined implies that you've lost all value to the world."

"A little reckless..." Kate repeated, as if she couldn't believe what she heard. "I've come to you after three days in a rake's bed."

Miss Donald didn't even blink. "And very nice it was, too, I'm sure. But that doesn't mean that you're fated to give up on virtue altogether." She settled a shrewd glance on Shelburn. "Does it, young man?"

Under that searching regard, Shelburn found himself shifting from one foot to the other. It was years since anybody had referred to him as a young man in that precise tone. He now knew where Kate had learned that ability to pierce through to the essence of a fellow with one glance. "I'd appreciate the opportunity for a word alone with Miss Starr."

What the deuce was wrong with him? He sounded like a gormless stripling requesting permission to court his sweetheart. He might even be blushing.

An approving smile lifted Miss Donald's lips. "You're most welcome to use my garden."

Kate observed this interchange with a puzzled frown. "Thank you, Donny." She paused. "I should introduce you two."

"No need." Shelburn returned his hostess's smile. He was yet to establish a satisfactory understanding with his lady, but he had the unshakable impression that Miss Donald already had his measure. "This is Miss Donald, who was governess to you and your sister Sylvie."

Kate's eyes went misty. "You remembered my sister's name?"

He shrugged. "Of course. I remember everything you've told me."

For a blazing instant, her gaze met his and he read exactly what he wanted to see. But before he could be sure, her eyelashes fluttered down to hide her expression.

"And you're Lord Shelburn," Miss Donald said. "Who hasn't always been a good man—"

"The worst lord in London, in fact," Kate murmured.

Miss Donald ignored the interjection. "But anyone can mend their ways, if they wish. The worst lord in London doesn't have to be a hopeless case."

By God, he didn't. His smile widened. "Indeed."

This meeting with Miss Donald was a revelation. The older woman reflected so many of the qualities that he admired in Kate. The unflappable calmness. The intelligence. The strength of character. The dry humor.

"Which is why I'm more than happy to lend you two my garden to sort yourselves out. I have a feeling that you've gone at everything topsy-turvy. But that doesn't mean your situation is hopeless either."

He bowed to the lady with genuine respect. "Thank you."

Miss Donald led them down the passage to a neat parlor, with doors opening onto a lush garden. The cottage was a substantial property for a woman who had worked for her living. Shelburn had a feeling that she might have left the Starr household with a generous bonus.

Miss Donald gestured toward a wooden bench under a flowering cherry tree. "You'll be private there. The neighbors are too far away to eavesdrop. Take your time, then come back inside when you're ready."

"Thank you, Donny." Kate kissed her governess's wrinkled cheek. "You're a treasure."

"Oh, away with you, lassie." For the first time, a trace of Scottish brogue infiltrated Miss Donald's crisp vowels. "You're a good girl, and a clever one. You'll find your path, I have no doubt."

Kate frowned. "I'm not sure I am a good girl."

"Your heart's in the right place. It won't lead you astray."

Kate didn't look entirely convinced about that either, but she let her governess go without trying to make her linger.

Shelburn descended the steps from the back of the house and extended his hand. "Come, my love. We have things to decide."

Kate's doubtful expression deepened. "Do we?"

"Oh, yes."

To his relief, she accepted his hand and followed him down onto the grass. Despite some encouraging signs, he wasn't yet reconciled to the way she'd left him. He thought that he knew why she had – birdbrained as the reason was – but until she told him what had been in her mind, he couldn't be at ease.

Knowing Kate, she would tell him. Despite this morning's flit, subterfuge wasn't her way, thank heaven.

Keeping hold of her hand, he brought her across to the bench, only releasing her once she sat down. When he didn't take his place beside her, she glanced up with an uncertain expression. "Aren't you going to join me?"

"I need to stand, I think." He felt like he'd swallowed a volcano, the emotions seething inside him were so ferocious.

Kate linked her hands in her lap. He'd noticed that she did that when she was nervous. "You must wonder about the scene you walked in on."

Now that he'd chased those interfering fools away, he didn't give a rat's arse about anything except working out his next step with Kate. But he could see that she wanted to tell him, and recounting recent events might help her to settle. She was as brittle as overcooked toffee and watching him with a world of questions in her lovely eyes.

"You seemed to be in trouble."

"I was." She paused. "You might be the worst lord in London, but it turns out that my affair with you saved me from marrying someone who is genuinely evil."

Despite Shelburn's eagerness to discuss their future, that focused his attention. "That bastard Williams?"

She nodded, and he caught a shadow of lingering horror in her face. "He and my cousin Alfred had cooked up a scheme to have me declared unfit, once the marriage took place. Williams wanted to take over the mills, with Alfred running them day to day. I assume I'd have been locked up in a madhouse, although they were kind enough to say that I'd be cared for."

The blistering irony in her tone made him flinch. What she told him was abominable. By God, Shelburn wished he'd beaten both those mongrels to a pulp, instead of letting them slink away with their tails between their legs. "That's unspeakable."

"It is." She managed a shaky smile, and he realized that she was coming to terms with the betrayal. That didn't cool his outrage. If he could, he'd cut off his hand to save her suffering the smallest hurt. "Thank you so much for showing up and sending them away. Things were about to turn nasty when you arrived and added your lofty consequence to the mix on my side."

"Any time," he said in a light tone, although he meant what he said.

"Coming up with that ridiculous claim that I was your intended bride was the perfect way to put them in their place." Her smile became more certain, and the strain faded from her features. "You were clever to think of it."

He stepped closer to the bench, as his heart gave a great thump. Battle was joined at last. He prayed that he prevailed.

While he was a man of overweening self-confidence, he was never sure of anything when it came to Kate. Yet the damnable dilemma was that for the first time, his interactions with a woman mattered.

Shelburn knew that cast an unfavorable light on his character. An unfavorable light that he was afraid revealed the painful truth that the worst lord in London really was unworthy of this glorious creature.

Take heart, man. Miss Donald thinks you're equal to the task.

Hell, he hoped to Jericho that Kate did.

He swallowed to moisten a mouth dry with nerves. Even so, his voice contained a humiliating crack when he spoke. "Damn it, Kate, what if it was more than just a ridiculous claim?"

CHAPTER EIGHTEEN

"It meant that Alfred let me go and..." Kate stopped, fearing that she must be losing her mind. "What on earth did you say?"

She must have misheard. Or perhaps Leighton was making a joke. In no universe that she inhabited could the rakish Lord Shelburn contemplate spending a lifetime with mundane Kate Starr.

To her astonishment, he didn't laugh or wave away his question. Instead, he dropped to one knee and took one of her hands. "Miss Starr – Kate – would you do me the inestimable honor of consenting to become my wife?"

She ripped her hand out of his and regarded him with a mixture of anger and dismay. Anger because she'd give up her hope of heaven to hear those words – if he truly meant them, when she knew he didn't. Dismay because he must feel like killing her because she brought him to such a pass.

"You don't have to do this." Her voice was flat. "I'm rich enough to live down any scandal, and nobody in your world will care if you seduced a peasant like me."

He frowned, looking haughty and displeased and so blasted tempting that she wanted to fling herself into his arms and beg him to kiss her. "I'm not asking you to marry me because I have to. I'm asking because I want to."

"No, you don't."

With an awkwardness that surprised her, he lurched to his feet. In general, he moved with the smoothness of a cat. Sheer relief must be affecting his balance. How he must have dreaded the prospect of his proposal meeting with consent.

"Give me the courtesy of accepting that I know my own mind," he bit out.

Her voice remained dull, as she told herself that she could survive this awful moment. Misery couldn't kill her. She'd proven that over and over. "You're just trying to be chivalrous, and I promise that you don't have to be. We both understood the arrangement when we came together. I'm not about to make a scene and demand you restore my honor."

She'd imagined that he'd appreciate her cooperation, but his expression turned even more thunderous. Which was odd, because most of the time, he was an easygoing man.

"What about all that stuff you said?"

Heat flooded her cheeks. She knew what he was referring to, although she wished that she didn't. While she might have spent the happiest days of her life with him, his brusque dismissal of her *tendre* continued to smart.

Curse him, now she had mortification to add to the other horrid emotions stewing inside her. "My confession of a girlish penchant? You talked me out of that in no uncertain terms, if you recall."

His dark stare was so intense, it burned. "That sounded like more than a girlish penchant. It sounded like a confession of love."

Oh, plague take the rogue. Did he mean to strip away every shred of her pride? She shifted on the bench and tried to avoid that magnetic stare.

"If it was love, it was for a man who doesn't exist. I'll admit that over these last, difficult years, I did find comfort in the fantasy of a perfect knight, who was kind and steadfast and true." She adopted an airy tone to dismiss any notion that after they parted, she might wear the willow for him. "I know you're not that man. You've never been that man. I bear you no resentment over that. These last few days, the man you are has been more than adequate for my purposes."

While her cheeks felt like they were on fire, Leighton had gone stark white. As he glared at her as if she'd offered him a deadly insult, an erratic muscle jerked in one lean cheek.

"But, Kate, what if I want to be that man?" His voice shook with the violence of his emotions. "What if knowing you has changed me forever, has shown me what fulfillment means? What if I want to be that perfect knight? At least for you."

What on earth? She must be gaping at him as if she lost her wits. None of this made sense. "But you said—"

"I damn well know what I said." His hand sliced the air. "I was an idiot. But you already know that. Or at least I was an idiot then. It didn't take me long to wake up to what a miracle fate had dropped undeserved into my lap. While I've been an arrogant ass and all kinds of blockhead, I'm not ready to let you go. I'll never be ready to let you go."

Never let her go? She struggled to claw back her common sense, to tell herself that he couldn't mean it.

But by all that was holy, he sounded like he meant it. He looked like he meant it. This desperate, ardent man was a million miles distant from the drawling, sardonic rake who had invited her into his carriage at the Angel.

God help her, she was in a terrible way. Both versions of Leighton were far too beguiling for her own good.

"You don't have to marry me." She hid her trembling hands in her skirts so they didn't reach for him. "I've said I'll come away with you."

He attempted a smile. Not a very successful one. "Miss Donald won't like that."

She wouldn't. "She has no say over what I do."

"Don't you want to marry me, Kate?" The naked hurt on his face made her wince.

"We're not—"

"Hell, why the devil would you?" Before she could answer, his face contorted in anguish, and he began to pace across the grass in fast, agitated strides. "Not now that you've found out what I'm really like. You've discovered how wrong you were about me all these years. It's no surprise that you don't want a bar of me."

"I've already said—"

He growled over the interruption. "Oh, I'm fine to share your bed. That at least I can do. But why would a smart woman want to spend the rest of her life with such a scurvy fellow as me? I'm not good enough. I've never been good enough. Even if I'd give my right arm to be worthy of you. You might have loved the fantasy Earl of Shelburn, but you've fallen altogether out of love with the real man."

"Don't be a fool, Leighton," she snapped. In her opinion, there had been quite enough drama already today.

"I am a fool. I'm *your* fool. Not that it does me an ounce of good."

"For pity's sake, stop feeling sorry for yourself. Of course I love you."

As suddenly as if he'd crashed into a pane of glass, Leighton stopped on the point of swinging to cross in front of her again. Taking his time, he turned to face her. His expression was brilliant with what she could only read as jubilation. "Devil take you, say that one more time."

Kate struggled upright on shaky legs, so shaky that she wasn't sure that they'd carry her if she wanted to run away. Although she'd already run away from him once today. She wasn't sure that she could muster the will to run away from him ever again. "Don't make me repeat it."

He frowned in confusion and stepped closer. "If you love me, why the hell did you sneak off?"

She made a forlorn gesture, cut short when he seized her hand. His touch felt possessive. She'd sunk so far from independent, willful Kate Starr that she adored the unequivocal claim he made on her. "I left you a note."

He grimaced again, this time in disgust. "You know what you can do with that."

She met eyes blazing with hurt, although hurting him had never been her intention. "I expressed my good wishes," she said in a reedy voice.

"And that was all you said. You could have been talking to a tradesman or a servant, not the man who had held you in his arms for three unforgettable days."

Kate thought back to that horrid moment when she'd faced a blank sheet of paper at the desk in the

Merry Haymaker's best parlor, empty and rather bleak at that hour of the morning. She bit her lip with guilt as she recalled her inadequate message.

I wish you well.

Nothing more. She hadn't even signed it.

Remembered misery thickened her voice. "I could either say nothing or far too much."

"And you didn't care how I might feel?"

Wondering, she surveyed his dark, intense features, seeing and hating the wound that she'd inflicted. Yet too astounded to believe what he seemed to be trying to tell her. "I didn't think you'd care."

"After what we'd come to mean to each other?"

"I didn't know we had. Or at least I didn't know what you felt."

She still didn't, not everything. But some mad, ridiculous spark lit inside her.

He shook his head, and wounded feelings abruptly dissolved into a rueful fondness. "I told you I was besotted."

Besotted? Yes, he had, hadn't he?

It wasn't love, but it was a start. A good start. Hope surged, even as she chided herself not to start building castles in the air. "You might say that to all your mistresses."

"Kate, Kate, Kate." He tightened his hold on her hand and carried it to his lips for a gentle kiss. She could see that he hadn't quite forgiven her for deserting him, but he was coming around. "To think I've always called you clever. Can't you tell the difference between self-serving nonsense and genuine esteem?"

That kiss on her knuckles made her head swim. "Not...not when I was so desperate for you to love me. I couldn't let myself believe anything you said.

Apart from the warning at the start. That I made sure I remembered."

"Oh, my darling..." Lucky for her doubtful balance, he placed his hands on her waist. Mere inches separated them now. "I forget how inexperienced you are with men. But your actions this morning were badly done. You didn't even say goodbye."

She twined her arms around his waist and buried her face in his chest, taking a deep breath of his spicy scent. Despite reminding herself that Kate Starr never cried, she blinked away tears.

Her answer emerged as a choked mutter. "I knew if I did, I'd make a fool of myself. And staying meant I'd only fall deeper in love, when I was already so in love with you that I didn't know how I was ever going to crawl back up into the air again."

"I'll see that you never climb out." Leighton's arms drew her against his body. "What would you have written in the note, if you'd said everything you held back?"

She tilted her face and met his gaze. She'd spent three days telling herself that she couldn't risk mistaking that glow in his eyes for anything except desire – and fleeting desire at that. Now perhaps, it might be time to discern more than lust there.

Her pride gave one last squeak at how she was about to lay herself open, but she ignored it. It was too late to protect herself. She had a feeling that it had been too late when she'd stepped into his carriage what felt like a lifetime ago, even if it was a mere three days.

Kate swallowed to ease the constriction in her throat, and her voice emerged low, but resonant with sincerity. "I would have said that I fell in love with you when I was sixteen and I've never wavered since. These last days have only confirmed that my heart knew what it wanted then and it knows what it wants now. I love you, Leighton. I'm yours for as long as you'll have me."

When his emotions were engaged, he went pale. Now he was as white as paper.

"Kate..." Leighton swept her up for a desperate kiss that blazed with the memory of all that they'd shared over these last extraordinary days.

For the first time, Kate surrendered the last corner of her soul. What was the point of holding back? She'd always been his, no matter how hard she'd struggled against giving him everything she was.

The kiss ventured beyond carnal heat into something more profound, something eternal. When at last he raised his head, they both looked shaken.

"My wonderful, wild girl..." He stared down at her as if she was the most glorious sight on earth. "What is it? Why are you crying?"

Kate blinked to shift the fog in front of her eyes. "I never cry."

"I can see that." He cupped her cheek, and the tenderness in his touch just strengthened her urge to weep. "There's nothing to cry about, my darling. We're together, and we're going to stay that way."

While she hadn't yet agreed to his proposal, he must know that she never wanted to leave him. "It's just...it's just that this morning, I was so unhappy."

"And you haven't had an easy time of it here with Williams and your cousins. No wonder you're a bit overwhelmed."

"They don't matter." She bit back a strangled sob. "But when I left the inn, I was sure that I'd never see you again. Then you descend on this house like an avenging angel and make everything right."

He gave a grunt of self-derisive amusement. "I doubt anyone has ever called me an angel before."

"I thought you were an angel when you danced with Sylvie."

His expression turned grave. "I should have danced with you as well. We needn't have waited so long to find each other then."

"You wouldn't have liked that at all. You would have missed out on all the fun." She was sure her smile was misty, as she dared to tease him. "You've so enjoyed being the worst lord in London."

"Without doubt, I've made the most of my rakish youth." He remained serious. "But those days are over forever. The worst lord in London is about to retire without a qualm. Instead, I plan to become the best husband in England."

What a lovely promise. "Oh, Leighton…"

He frowned. "You are going to accept me, aren't you, Kate? I couldn't bear it if you sent me away."

"I'll never send you away." She rose up on her toes – how nice that she had to do that – and kissed him with all the love in her heart. "I love you."

Joy transfigured his face, wiped away all trace of the cynicism that she'd once thought was his essence. "So it's yes?"

"Yes, yes, yes." She punctuated each acceptance with a quick kiss.

"My love!" He cradled her face in his hands. This time when she kissed him, she didn't get away so fast.

By the time Kate wafted back to the real world, she and Leighton were sitting on the bench, holding hands and staring at each other with euphoric incredulity. "My life has changed in just three days. Last Sunday, I was set to marry that lout Jebediah Williams and settle for what I could have, instead of what I wanted. Now I feel like all my dreams are coming true. Is this really happening?"

"It is. Believe it." Affection warmed Leighton's laugh. "Now, sweetheart, we need to make some plans. Would you like to stay with Miss Donald, while I go to London and arrange a special license? I'd like to take you with me, but I think it's wiser if we try and avoid a scandal. After all, you're about to become the Countess of Shelburn."

Her? A countess? It seemed too outlandish. "I like the sound of that."

"Get used to it. We can be married as soon as I return. I hope by the end of the week."

"Oh, my dear." She leaned in for another kiss. She couldn't get enough of his kisses. This morning, she'd been convinced that she'd never experience the wonder of his kiss again. "So soon?"

He shrugged. "I intend to claim you as mine in front of the whole world. Anyway, I know what I want and I think you do, too. Why should we delay?"

"What about the mills?"

He gave another brief laugh. "What the devil do I want with a roomful of oversized, rattling machinery? I'll have my solicitor draw up an agreement that all your property remains yours to manage as you wish."

She studied him. "But you don't know how rich I am."

"I'm not short of a penny myself. Our children will want for nothing."

He kept stealing the breath from her. "Children?"

"God willing." He flattened one hand over her midriff. "Perhaps you already carry my baby. We weren't careful at the Merry Haymaker."

A surge of almost unbearably powerful emotion made her heart expand almost to bursting. She placed a shaking hand on his, pressing his palm against the place where a son or daughter might grow. "I'd love to have your child."

This time, his kiss held as much reverence as passion. "We're going to create a family, sweetheart."

"A family..."

"You're going to cry again, aren't you?"

She lifted a hand to dash stinging moisture from her eyes. "I've so missed having someone to love. All this just seems like too much." She stared at him. "You know that the world will say you've made a dreadful mésalliance, mingling your blue-blooded magnificence with a peasant like me."

His lips turned down in dismissal. "What do I care what those useless fribbles say?"

"You didn't care when you danced with Sylvie."

"I didn't, and I don't care now." His smile was alive with the quicksilver charm that she so loved. "Anyway, I'm not marrying a peasant. I'm marrying a goddess."

It was Kate's turn to laugh. "I fear that once you live with me day to day, you'll discover that I'm a mere human."

"Never. The woman I love isn't a mere anything."

Kate's heartbeat stopped. She felt like the entire world stopped. "You...you never said you loved me."

"How could I not love you?" He frowned. "Don't tell me you've been fretting about that, you silly widgeon."

"I have," she admitted, tightening her grip on his hand.

"You had me head over heels, even before I acted like such a pompous buffoon and told you not to complicate things with emotion. It took my head a day or so to catch up with my heart, I'll admit. But after our first night together, I knew you were the one for me. I thought – hoped – you felt the same.”

“I did. I do.” She sucked in a shaky breath. “But sometimes, it's nice to have the actual words to hang onto.”

She prepared for gentle mockery, but he looked more earnest than she'd ever seen him. He lifted her hand and held it against his pounding heart. “I love you, Kate. I will always love you. I've never said those words to another woman. It took me a long time to find the one person who could make me a better man. I dedicate all that I am to you, now and forever.”

With a tenderness that set her heart alight with joy and hope, he drew her into his arms. His kiss was a fervent pledge of a love that she knew would last forever.

EPILOGUE

Bradbourne, Derbyshire, November 1819

Kate worked in her office at Starr Mills, high above the large, airy weaving rooms on the lower floors. Lamps lit the space, and a fire blazed in the hearth. Winter had come early this year. Snow lay thick on the steep hills encircling the valley where she'd grown up.

How she loved these rare moments when she had the mill to herself. After the machines fell silent and the workers all returned to their snug houses in the surrounding village.

She scribbled a few remarks on the building plans spread out before her on the desk and when she looked up, Leighton was standing in the doorway. His smile spoke of the unshakable love that after more than three years of marriage, she claimed as her due.

Snowflakes dusted the shoulders of his black greatcoat and the brim of his stylish hat. He was as handsome as ever. More so. These days, Leighton looked much younger than the world-weary libertine she'd first met. Contentment had banished the hint of cynicism that had once shadowed his expression.

"Good evening, my love," she said softly, as her heart did its usual dance of happiness at the sight of him.

She thought that she'd known what love was when she wed him in Heddle End's ancient stone church. The ceremony took place two days after he proposed, and Donny and the vicar's wife had been their only witnesses. But every day since had deepened her adoration for her husband.

He moved into the room, taking off his gloves and coat and hat and tossing them onto a chair. "I thought I'd come down and escort you home."

Kate stretched to loosen stiff muscles and saw with surprise that it was past seven. "That would be lovely."

These days, the house that she'd grown up in was once again a home, full of love and laughter. As was Leighton's grand and ancient manor house in Devon. She'd come to realize that wherever she and her husband were together, there was her home.

He prowled around to stand behind her and drop a kiss on top of her head. Even now, these casual gestures of affection never failed to delight her. "That's me. Lovely."

His sardonic response made her laugh. "Well, it is."

"Don't tell anyone." He rested one hand on her shoulder. "I have a reputation as a wild and dangerous rake to keep up."

"Not these days."

"No, not these days." His response contained no trace of regret. "Are those the designs for the new school?"

"Yes. I think we're finally getting closer to what we want. At this rate, we should be able to start construction in the spring."

"So everything will be up and running by the time the baby comes."

"Yes." Kate rested one hand on her midriff, where their second child nestled. At this early stage, her pregnancy hardly showed. So far, only Leighton shared the sweet secret. "We have a lot to look forward to, don't we?"

He squeezed her shoulder. "We do indeed."

And so many wonderful things to look back on as well. It had been a busy, fulfilling, joyous three years, even if she and Leighton had needed to make a few adjustments along the way.

Kate had to learn how to become a countess, however unconventional, and chatelaine of Leighton's many properties, most daunting of all the family seat at Capstone Abbey. Leighton had to fit the requirements of running the mills into his life.

That had ended up being less onerous than she'd feared, because the new management structure at the factory allowed the Shelburns time for their other commitments. Just after Alfred's departure, Kate had promoted a couple of promising workers from the floor to help run the enterprise. One was even a woman, which had raised eyebrows at first but had proven a great success in the long run.

To her surprise, and she suspected his, Leighton had soon developed an avid interest in the factory. These days they spent at least as much time talking about her thriving business as discussing their activities as Lord and Lady Shelburn.

The marriage of one of the kingdom's most eligible bachelors to a fabulously wealthy mill owner had raised eyebrows in high society, too – raised eyebrows seemed to be *de rigueur* when it came to the Shelburns. But after a lifetime of reading about the beau monde, Kate had enjoyed her seasons in London, and she found Leighton's parliamentary activities fascinating.

Her duplicitous cousins, thank heaven, had disappeared from her life. Once it became obvious that Kate was adamant about withdrawing all support, Alfred and Hazel had taken ship for America. She had no idea what had become of them since.

Nor had Jebediah Williams prospered. It turned out that he was nowhere near as solvent as he'd claimed. A year ago, he'd lost his factories and mines amidst a morass of debt and bad management.

"With the new infirmary and school in operation, the workers will be so happy that productivity at Starr Mills will surge," Leighton said.

"I hope so." Kate twisted around far enough to see her husband. "At least my productivity is on track. I feel so disgustingly well this time."

During her first pregnancy, she'd suffered from bad morning sickness. She only had to think back to her husband's kindness and patience through those difficult months to know that he was as committed to their union as she was. In truth, he had been a perfect knight then, although he'd scoffed whenever she'd told him that.

She supposed that perfect knights were by nature uncomfortable with praise.

Her perfect knight was still smiling. "The result of our earlier productivity is looking forward to meeting his new brother or sister."

"Richard mightn't feel the same when he's no longer the sole focus of attention."

"He'll cope. He's an angel, after all."

A snort of laughter escaped Kate, as her hand covered Leighton's where it rested on her shoulder. "You must be talking about another child altogether. He's been disrupting our world from the moment he was conceived."

Their three days at the Merry Haymaker had created a baby, or at least so they'd always believed. Their dark-haired, spirited, squalling son had arrived just short of nine months after their wedding. And ever since, he'd been running them ragged.

"At least right now he's disrupting his grandmother's world."

For this short trip north to the mill, they'd left Richard with Leighton's mother in Surrey. The Dowager Countess of Shelburn had welcomed Kate as a daughter-in-law, although she should have been horrified to learn that her son chose a woman of no pedigree. Leighton's mother had later confided that seeing him fall in love at last had been a huge relief. From the moment that she heard about the wedding, she'd been eager to meet the lady who had captured the earl's once unassailable heart.

One of the loveliest things about marrying Leighton meant that Kate became part of an extended family, made up of his sisters and their husbands and children. Not to mention a throng of cousins, all much nicer than Hazel and Alfred. Richard and the new baby would grow up surrounded by people who loved them.

"Now, his grandmother really does think Richard is an angel," Kate said. "Little Lord Lemaire can do no wrong in her eyes."

"Whereas with a hellion for a mother and a rake, even if reformed, for a father, he promises to keep us on our toes."

"I like an interesting life."

"Hmm," Leighton said, although she heard the warmth underlying his noncommittal answer. He idolized his son and took pride in the boy's energy and intelligence, even if they had to cope with occasional mischief, too.

Kate bundled up the designs and pushed back her chair to stand and face her husband. But instead of moving aside, Leighton crowded her until her rump hit the desk.

When she raised her head, she met eyes alight with a purpose that had become very familiar over the last few years. "Leighton?"

He placed his hands on her waist. "You know, I've never enjoyed you on the desk."

She rolled her eyes, although as ever, the heat in his gaze set her wanton blood rushing. "Of course you have. I don't think there's a desk in the whole Anstey patrimony that hasn't seen me under you. Or over you. Or beside you. I've been face up, I've been face down. Good heavens, I've even been upside down. In the last three years, I've performed acrobatics on more blasted desks than I care to count."

Not that she minded. The desire that fueled their first encounters had only become stronger and richer as time went on.

His low chuckle always made her skin prickle with sensual need. "Poor you."

His exaggerated sympathy made her smile. Because they both knew that she reveled in his powerful hunger for her.

"We've almost been caught half a dozen times." The household staff had soon learned to knock before they entered a room.

"There's nobody here now."

A thrill sizzled through her, as she glanced around as if to confirm what he said. The office was on the top floor of the tallest building in Bradbourne. Their privacy was more assured here than it was at Capstone Abbey. "No, there's not."

"And while I might have taken advantage of you on other desks, I haven't taken advantage of you on this particular desk."

Kate's eyebrows arched, even as her lips curled in greedy anticipation. "It's not a challenge, you know. You don't need to molest me on every desk in England."

Not to mention the sofas and tables and carpets and window seats.

He shrugged. "A man needs something to fill his idle hours."

"He could take up gardening. Or bowls. Or woodwork. Or... *Oof!*"

His hold suddenly tightened, and she found herself sitting on the desk.

"He could. But pleasuring the woman I love is a much better use of my time than mucking around with a trowel or a hammer. It's—" He broke off. "What?"

Kate blinked, realizing that she must be staring at him the way her gormless sixteen-year-old self had stared at him at Rushby Hall. "You called me the woman you love."

The humorous impatience in his expression did nothing to mask his lascivious intentions. "What the devil else am I going to call you?"

One hand made a helpless gesture. "I know you love me, but I always like to hear it."

"I love you, Kate." This time his voice turned gruff with sincerity.

Her heart flipped over in her chest in the disconcerting way that she should be used to by now. "And I love you, Leighton."

He lashed his arms about her and kissed her with an intoxicating mixture of sweetness and craving that melted her blood to hot syrup. When he bunched up her skirts, she parted her legs to allow him closer. As he gently lowered her onto the desk, she ignored the rustles and rattles and crashes as he cleared the space for her.

"Now I know why you took off your outdoor clothes," she said, tunneling her hand through his thick black hair.

His lips twitched. "You should have guessed then that I had seduction in mind."

"Lucky me."

His smile intensified. "No, lucky me. My wife all to myself, a cold night, a warm room, and a fresh desk to ravish you upon. What more could a man want?"

Despite her surging excitement, she clicked her tongue in mock disapproval. "You're such a reprobate."

"Only with you, my darling. Only with you."

"Oh, Leighton, I love it when you say things like that." Kate sighed and tugged at his neckcloth to bring him down over her. "Now let's not waste a very fine desk that's begging for us to take advantage of it. Fly me to paradise, my beloved husband."

"With the utmost pleasure, my lovely wife," Leighton said with a lightness that his passionate kiss belied, as his mouth took hers in a silent message of eternal devotion.

ABOUT THE AUTHOR

Australian Anna Campbell has written 11 multi award-winning historical romances for Avon HarperCollins and Grand Central Publishing. As an independently published author, she's released more than 30 bestselling stories. Right now, she is working on a new series called Scoundrels of Mayfair, set amidst the glamour and sensuality of Regency London. Anna has won numerous awards for her stories, including RT Book Reviews Reviewers Choice, the Booksellers Best, the Golden Quill (three times), the Heart of Excellence (twice), the Write Touch, the Aspen Gold (twice), and the Australian Romance Readers' favorite historical romance (five times).

Anna loves to hear from her readers. You can find her at:

Website: www.annacampbell.com

facebook.com/AnnaCampbellFans

twitter.comAnnaCampbellOz

bookbub.com/authors/anna-campbell

The Worst Lord in London: Scoundrels of Mayfair Book 1

Headlong into the unknown...

Independent, willful Kate Starr has cherished a penchant for handsome Lord Shelburn since she was sixteen years old, but as a mill-owning industrialist, she moves in a different world from the libertine earl. Then one fateful day, Shelburn invites her to accompany him in a scandalous race, and immediate physical attraction swiftly turns into blazing passion.

The hunter caught...

Leighton Anstey, Earl of Shelburn, glories in his reputation as the worst lord in London. His fame as an irresistible seducer is unrivaled, although his amours are notable for their explosive heat, not their longevity. The dashing lord has never met a woman who can hold his wandering attention, until he tumbles into a liaison with a mysterious woman who enthrals him, body and soul.

A brief encounter or a forever love?

Neither Kate nor Shelburn views their torrid affair as more than a shooting star, flaring red-hot for a brilliant instant, then destined to fade to nothing. But does the fiery desire raging between them blind them to the chance of finding lifelong happiness together?

The Trouble with Earls:
Scoundrels of Mayfair Book 2

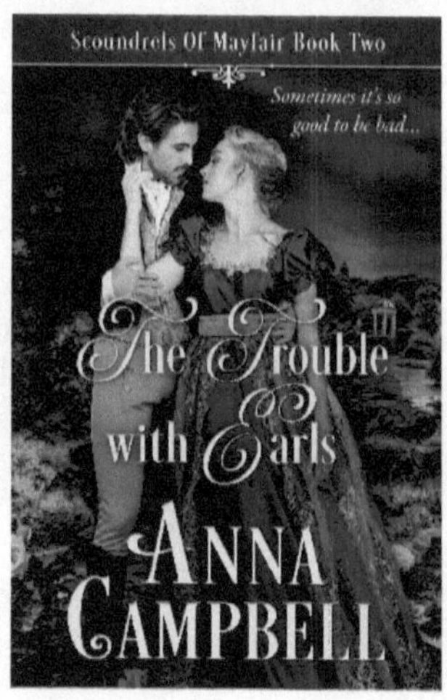

The wild rogue and the wallflower!

Toby Sutton, Earl of Renfrew, is a notorious libertine with no interest in marrying a wellbred young miss and making her his countess. But when he meets lovely Lady Viola Frain, irresistible desire creates an explosive mix with his native recklessness. Within a matter of days, he and Viola are joined in a hurried marriage of convenience, patched together to scotch an almighty scandal.

Marry in haste, repent at leisure?

With two spectacular older sisters, shy Viola Frain is used to being the overlooked member of the family. When handsome Lord Renfrew literally falls at her feet, Viola finally meets a man who thinks she's special. But before the fragile bloom of

attraction can flower, she finds herself wed to
Renfrew and whisked away to brooding Brazey
Castle, where shadows of old tragedy threaten her
frail hope of happiness.

The trouble with earls…

Society watches avidly, forecasting disaster for an
alliance between two people so mismatched. Can
passion unite the rake and the recluse? Or is the
truth just as Viola fears? That the trouble with earls
is that they're bound to break your heart.

The Last Duke She'd Marry: Scoundrels of Mayfair Book 3

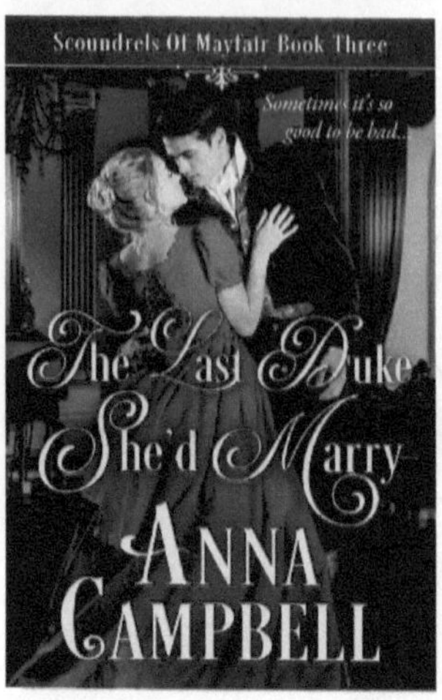

She wants to be a duchess. Just not HIS duchess!

Pure and proper Lady Juliet Frain was born to be a duchess. Everyone says so. Now society awaits the announcement of the elegant beauty's engagement to the dignified and honorable Duke of Granville. However all Juliet's plans go awry when she meets the scandalous but sinfully attractive Duke of Evesham. The wild libertine is the last man Juliet wants to find irresistible, yet somehow she can't keep her hands off him. And suddenly to her chagrin, nobody is calling Juliet either pure or proper!

He's no Romeo...

After ten riotous years on the Continent, Lucas
Hebden, Duke of Evesham, has returned to
London, trailing a well-earned reputation as a rake
and a reprobate. But an unexpected loss in a card
game finds him far from London's fleshpots and
playing at amateur dramatics in the country. Even
worse, he's starting to confuse the poetic passion in
Romeo and Juliet with the real-life passion that has
him pursuing his disapproving but breathtakingly
lovely leading lady. It's clear that Lady Juliet Frain
has no time for bad boys, and any sensible man
would give up – but then nobody ever called
Evesham sensible!

***When Juliet's suitor Granville arrives to
propose, it's the battle of the dukes! Once
the curtain falls, which duke will emerge
victorious and take the starring role in
Juliet's heart?***

Coming in 2023!

The Duke Says I Do:
Scoundrels of Mayfair Book 4

Portia's story! Coming early 2024.